Chloe

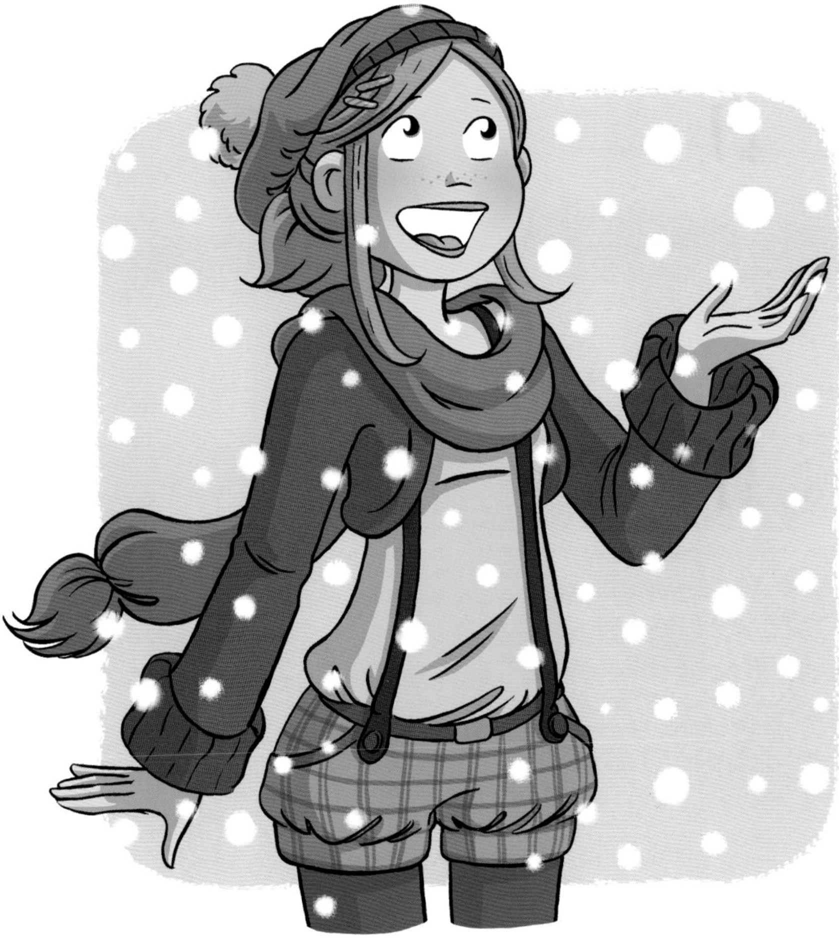

charmz™

MORE GRAPHIC NOVELS AVAILABLE FROM

Charmz™

COMING SOON!

Greg Tessier and Amandine
Chloe
The New Girl
charmz

CHLOE #1
"THE NEW GIRL"

Greg Tessier and Amandine
Chloe
The Queen of High School
charmz

CHLOE #2
"THE QUEEN
OF HIGH SCHOOL"

Sweeties
CHERRY SKYE
charmz

SWEETIES #1
"CHERRY SKYE"

GFFs
GHOST FRIENDS FOREVER
charmz

G.F.F.s #1
"GHOST FRIENDS
FOREVER"

COMING SOON!

STITCHED
MARIAH McCOURT
AARON ALEXOVICH
The First Day of the Rest of her Life
charmz

STITCHED #1
"THE FIRST DAY OF THE
REST OF HER LIFE"

STITCHED
MARIAH McCOURT • AARON ALEXOVICH
Love in the Time of Assumption
charmz

STITCHED #2
"LOVE IN THE TIME
OF ASSUMPTION"

PATRICIA LYFOUNG
The Scarlet Rose
charmz

SCARLET ROSE #1
"I KNEW I'D
MEET YOU"

Ana and the COSMIC RACE
AMY CHU
KATA KANE
THE RACE BEGINS
charmz

ANA AND THE
COSMIC RACE #1
"THE RACE BEGINS"

Charmz graphic novels are available for $9.99 in paperback, and $14.99 in hardcover.
Available from booksellers everywhere. You can also order online from www.papercutz.com.
Or call 1-800-886-1223, Monday through Friday, 9–5 EST. MC, Visa, and AmEx accepted.
To order by mail, please add $5.00 for postage and handling for first book ordered,
$1.00 for each additional book and make check payable to NBM Publishing.
Send to: Charmz, 160 Broadway, Suite 700, East Wing, New York, NY 10038.

Charmz graphic novels are also available wherever e-books are sold.

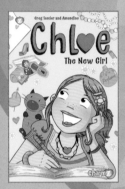

Chl♥e

The Queen of High School

Story by Greg Tessier
Art by Amandine

NEW YORK

Believing in your ideas also means defending them the best you can and in different ways! —
Thanks to my family and friends for their constant support!
—Greg

Thanks to all those who, through their support and encouragement, have accompanied Chloe
into 9th Grade.
A thousand thanks to Louna and Madd for their coloring help during the final production
stages, and a thousand more thanks to Pierre for his technical, moral, and culinary support!
—Amandine

Chl♥e

CHLOE #2
"The Queen of High School"

GREG TESSIER — Story
AMANDINE — Art and color
AMANDINE — Cover
JOE JOHNSON — Translation
BRYAN SENKA — Lettering
JEFF WHITMAN — Assistant Managing Editor
MARIAH McCOURT — Editor
JIM SALICRUP
Editor-in-Chief

Charmz is an imprint of Papercutz.

ISBN HC: 978-1-62991-834-1
ISBN PB: 978-1-62991-833-4

Printed in China
November 2017

Charmz books may be purchased for business or promotional use.
For information on bulk purchases please contact Macmillan
Corporate and Premium Sales Department at (800) 221-7945 x5442

Distributed by Macmillan
First Charmz Printing

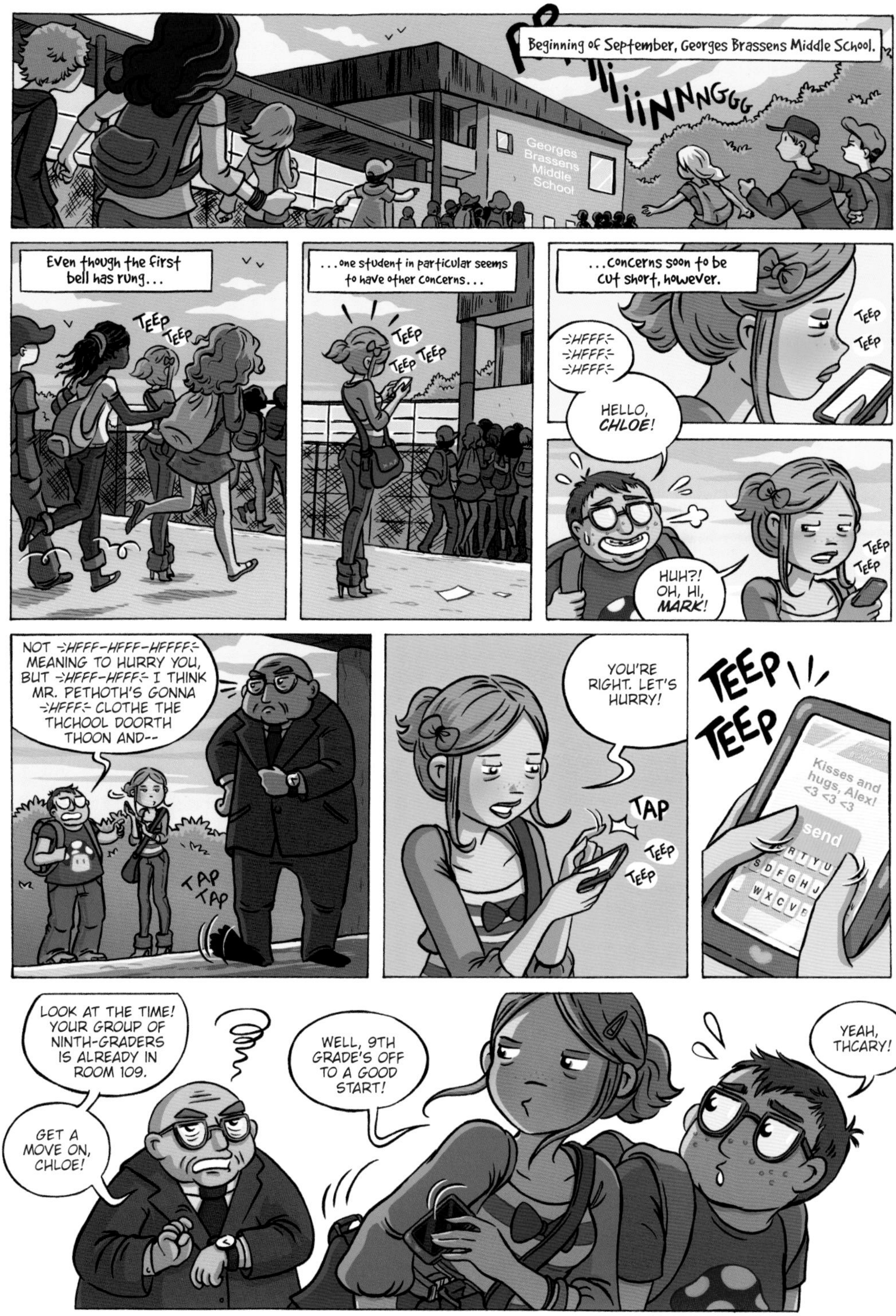

Beginning of September, Georges Brassens Middle School.
IINNNGGG
Georges Brassens Middle School
Even though the first bell has rung...
TEEP TEEP
...one student in particular seems to have other concerns...
TEEP TEEP TEEP
...concerns soon to be cut short, however.
HFFF HFFF HFFF
HELLO, CHLOE!
TEEP TEEP
HUH?! OH, HI, MARK!
TEEP TEEP
NOT HFFF-HFFF-HFFFF MEANING TO HURRY YOU, BUT HFFF-HFFF I THINK MR. PETHOTH'S GONNA HFFF CLOTHE THE THCHOOL DOORTH THOON AND--
TAP TAP
YOU'RE RIGHT. LET'S HURRY!
TAP
TEEP
TEEP
TEEP TEEP
Kisses and hugs, Alex! <3 <3 <3
send
LOOK AT THE TIME! YOUR GROUP OF NINTH-GRADERS IS ALREADY IN ROOM 109.
GET A MOVE ON, CHLOE!
WELL, 9TH GRADE'S OFF TO A GOOD START!
YEAH, THCARY!

Once inside the school, Chloe's welcome from the new students is very different than she expected...

CHECK HER OUT?!

WOW!

IS SHE A NINTH-GRADER, SIR?

SO CLASSY!

PFEF PFF

SHE'S SO SWANKY IN HEELS!

THOSE NINTH-GRADERS SURE ARE STYLISH!

PFF

THEY LOOK JUST LIKE ADULTS!

I'M A HUGE FAN!

PFFF

...much to her joy!

PFFF PFFF

SHE'S A REAL BEAUTY QUEEN.

THOSE ÷HHHH-HHH÷ LITTLE SIXTH-GRADERS HAVE GOOD TASTE!

PFF

HNN HNN

HEE HEE HEE!

PFF PFF

Exaggeration

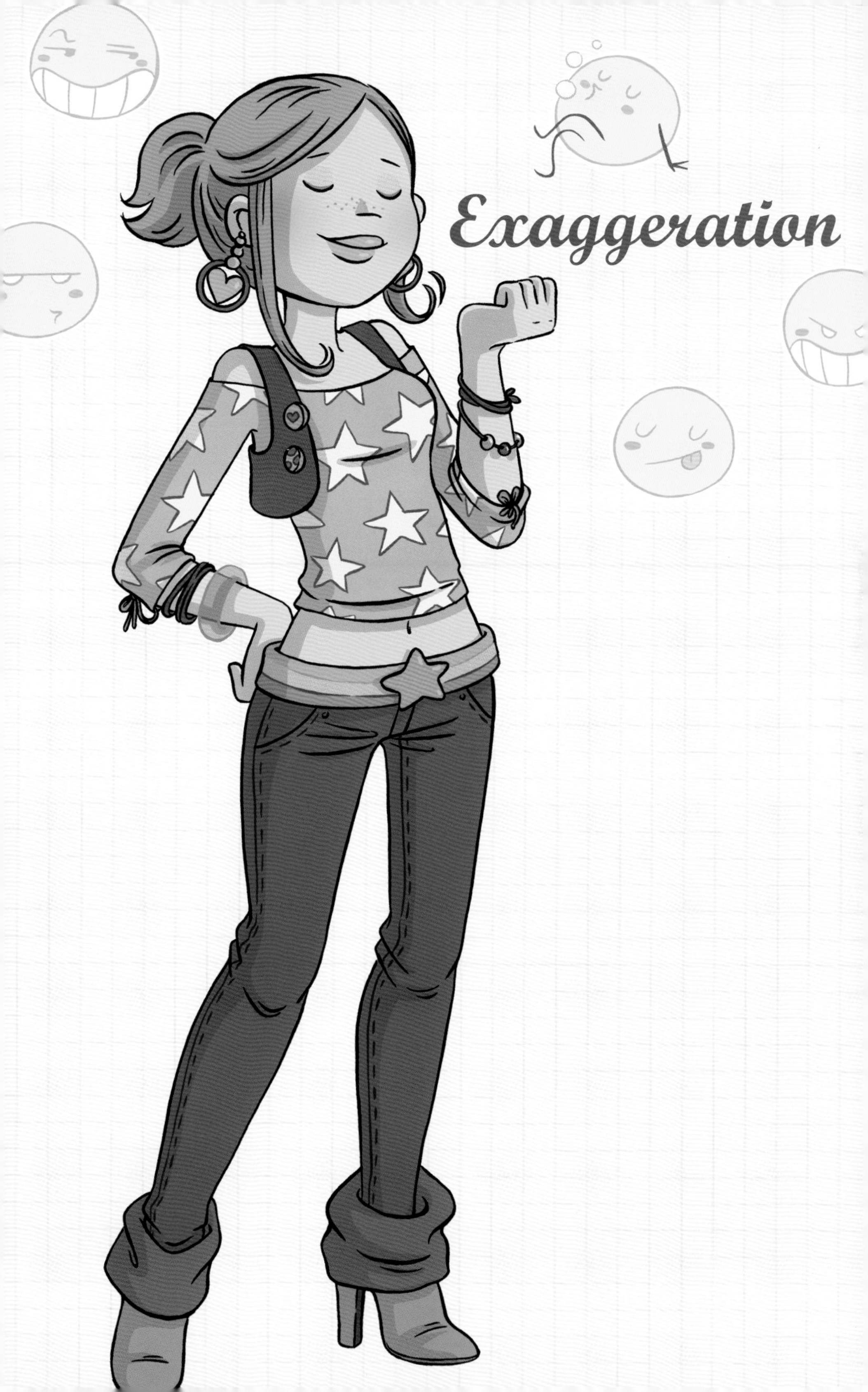

NOK
NOK

...

YOU GOTTA ASSERT YOURSELF, MARK! WE'RE IN 9TH GRADE NOW. KNOCK LOUD!

YOU SEE, LIKE TH--

BOING

!

YOU WON'T FIND ANYONE HERE, MISS! HA HA HA!

UH--

YOU CAN GO IN AND SIT DOWN. WE WERE WAITING FOR YOU!

Some things definitely haven't changed in the classroom, however...

LOOKS LIKE CHLOE'S BEHIND THE TIMES AGAIN!

...

SO, I'M **MISTER COSTA**! I'LL BE YOUR HOMEROOM TEACHER THIS YEAR.

I'LL ALSO BE TEACHING YOU HISTORY. IT'S MY FAVORITE SUBJECT.

I'M COUNTING ON YOU TO PUSH YOUR-SELVES TO THE ACADEMIC LIMIT AND RESPOND TO CURRENT EVENTS, OKAY?

COSTA

WELL, THAT KRUSTY THE CLOWN ISN'T RESPONDING TO CURRENT FASHION TRENDS WITH SHIRTS LIKE THAT! HA HA HA!

...this time, however, there was no guarantee her good habits would last for very long!

WHAT A WONDERFUL STATE OF MIND, **ANISSA**! SUCH REFLECTION, SUCH INTELLIGENCE! YOU'RE A FUTURE NOBEL PRIZE WINNER, FOR SURE!

JUST WHO DOES SHE THINK SHE IS? I DON'T THINK SHE KNOWS WHO SHE'S MESSING WITH!

"SHE," AS YOU PUT IT, IS **FATOUMA SIMBA**--

--DON'T TRY TO WALK ALL OVER HER 'CAUSE SHE CAN SET YOU STRAIGHT, WHEN NEEDED!

WHOA! THAT FATOUMA DOESN'T LOOK THAT EASY TO GET ALONG WITH, EITHER! IT'S GONNA BE FUN AND GAMES THIS YEAR.

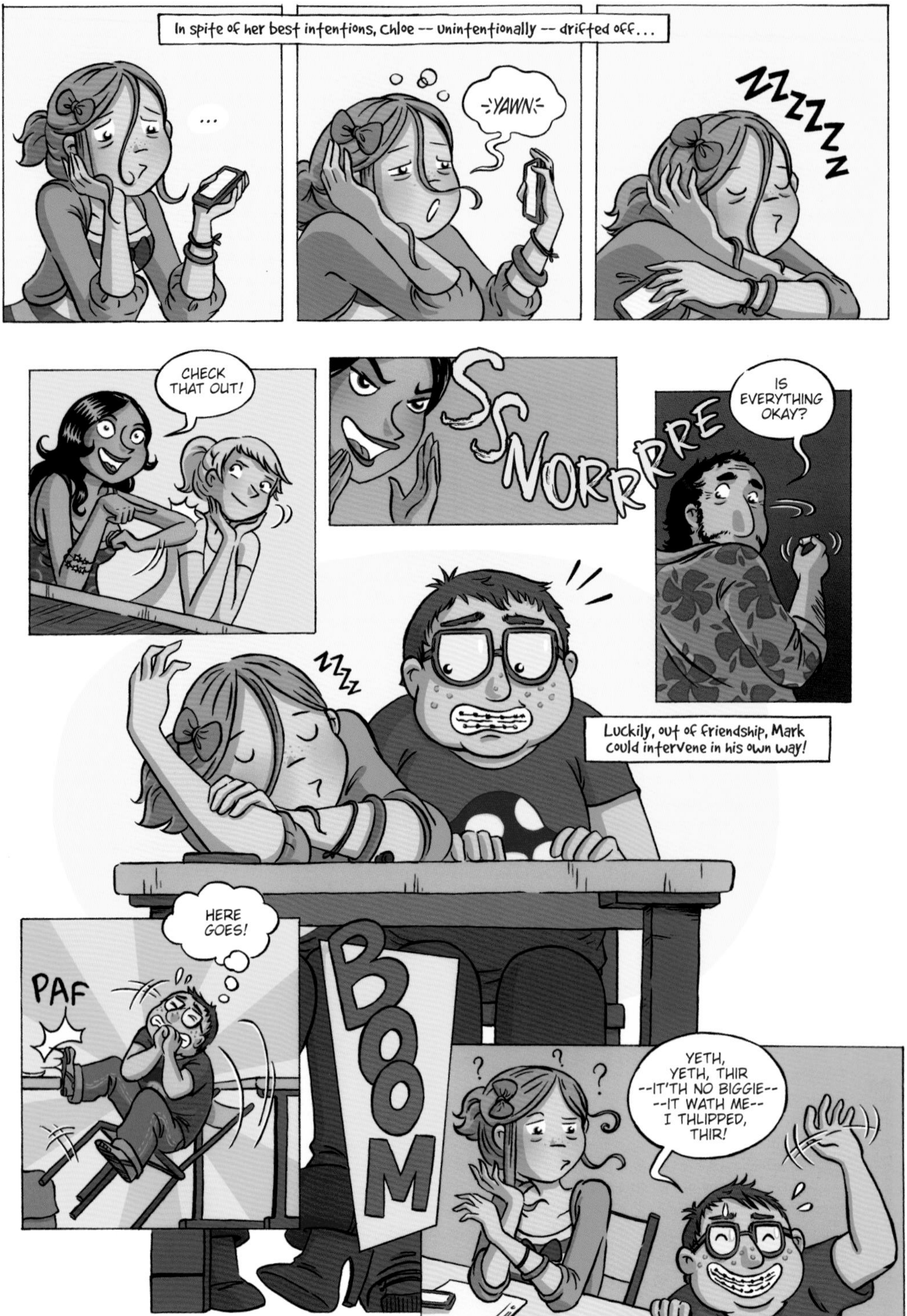
In spite of her best intentions, Chloe -- unintentionally -- drifted off...
...
-YAWN-
ZZZZZZ
CHECK THAT OUT!
SSNORRRRE
IS EVERYTHING OKAY?
ZZZZ
Luckily, out of friendship, Mark could intervene in his own way!
HERE GOES!
PAF
BOOM
? ? ?
YETH, YETH, THIR --IT'TH NO BIGGIE-- --IT WATH ME-- I THLIPPED, THIR!

CRRRIIIIIINGG

-YAWN-

I DON'T KNOW IF IT WATH THUCH A GOOD IDEA GIVING YOU ADVITHE ABOUT COMPUTERTH, AFTER ALL.

TEEP
TEEP TEEP
TEEP TEEP

FROM THE LOOKTH OF YOU, YOU PROBABLY THPENT MOTHT OF LATHT NIGHT IN FRONT OF YOUR COMPUTER THCREEN, DIDN'T YOU?

UH-- YES, MAYBE A LITTLE.

TEEP TEEP
TEEP

BUT YOU'RE HARDLY IN A POSITION TO BE LECTURING ME, ARE YOU?

OKAY, OKAY, THAT'TH FINE! IF THAT'TH HOW YOU WANT IT, YOU JUTHT MANAGE ON YOUR OWN THEN!

ESPECIALLY, WITH YOUR SUNGLASSES GIMMICK!

11

So, to get past this bit of unpleasantness, our young heroine decided she'd go see the sixth-graders she'd met that same morning during her lunch break.

TAP TEEP TAP

SHE'S LIKE A MODEL!

HEE HEE!

DID YOU SEE? SHE HAS THE LATEST CELLPHONE, TOO!

YOU!

ME? I DIDN'T DO ANYTHING!

HI, GIRLS!

BIP

UH-HELLO!

AHH! A MESSAGE FROM *ALEX*, MY BOYFRIEND.

TEE BELEEP

HE'S THINKING ABOUT HIS CHLOE! *HEE HEE!* HE'S IN 10TH GRADE AND--

IN 10TH GRADE?

SO LUCKY!

HMMM --HMMM-- A BLOG WITH FASHION ADVICE, THAT'S A GOOD IDEA.

YES! BUT, SINCE HE'S IN A BOARDING SCHOOL NOW, I ONLY SEE HIM ON WEEKENDS.

TAP TAP TEEDEEP

OH, NO! THAT'S TOO BAD!

YOUR OUTFIT'S REALLY PRETTY, THOUGH! I'D REALLY LIKE TO KNOW HOW TO DRESS LIKE YOU.

REALLY, IT'S NOT ALWAYS EASY TO CHOOSE THE RIGHT CLOTHES.

I'LL HAVE HUNDREDS OF FOLLOWERS, THAT'S FOR SURE.

COME BACK HERE!

RUN, RUN, IT'S *MIREILLE*!

OWW!

HEE HEE HEE HEE HEE HEE HEE HEE

TRIP

DON'T YOU TALK?

ELYSE, CHLOE JUST ASKED YOU A QUESTION?

UH ...YES... UH...

IT'S JUST EVERYTHING'S SO *DIFFERENT* HERE!

NOOOOO!

IT'S A BIG CHANGE, ISN'T IT? DON'T WORRY, THOUGH. IT'S TOTALLY NORMAL TO FEEL A BIT LOST WHEN YOU GO TO A NEW SCHOOL.

I WENT THROUGH THAT, TOO, NOT SO LONG AGO, YOU KNOW. I GET IT!

SO, FOR ALL THOSE REASONS, I'M GOING TO GIVE YOU A BIG GIFT! I'LL BE YOUR GUIDE AND SHOW YOU EVERY-THING THERE IS TO KNOW ABOUT THIS AWESOME MIDDLE SCHOOL.

UH, OKAY!

From then on, even though Chloe was full of good intentions...

IT'S SIMPLE, YOU SEE!

TO THE RIGHT, YOU HAVE THE CAFETERIA--

TO THE LEFT, THE COMMON ROOM--

...the attention bestowed upon her...

SHE'S OUR LEADER!

THANK YOU!

...soon went to her head!

OH! I'M SO TIRED...

DON'T GO ANYWHERE, CHLOE, WE'LL GET YOU SOME CEREAL BARS!

MMMMM-- YES, THAT'S GOOD! LIKE THAT, YES!

AS I WAS TELLING YOU, AN ELEGANT HAIRSTYLE GOES HAND IN HAND WITH AN ELEGANT OUTFIT! THAT'S BASIC, OH, YES!

At home, too, her parents seemed determined to boost her self-esteem to the max...

TAP TAP TAP

I DON'T KNOW MUCH ABOUT IT, BUT IT SURE SEEMS TO ME OUR CHLOE'S MANAGING LIKE A PRO!

...to the great despair of her little brother!

TAP TAP TAP

WHY CAN'T I PLAY ANY GAMES?

BECAUSE WE ALREADY TOLD YOU, ARTIE--

TAP TAP TAP

THIS TAKES LOTS OF TIME.

YOUR SISTER IS CREATING A BLOG. THAT'S LOTS OF WORK!

FOR EXAMPLE, I HAVE TO CHOOSE A HOME PAGE--

WHAT?

?

BUT YOU ALREADY HAVE A HOME WITH DADDY AND MOMMY! THIS IS YOUR HOME, ISN'T IT?

HA HA HA!

HEE HEE!

TAP TAP

FINE, IF THAT'S HOW IT IS, I'LL LEAVE YOU ALONE!

Feeling misunderstood, Artie decided to go seek his happiness elsewhere...

AGREED, ARTHUR?

BY THE END OF THE MONTH I WANT THIS PERMISSION SLIP SIGNED BY ONE OF YOUR PARENTS.

YES, MA'AM!

SEE YOU TOMORROW!

Arthur

NO ENTRY

NO MORE VIDEO GAMES! I'LL SPEND ALL MY TIME TAKING CARE OF YOU, *THINGUMABOB.*

I GOTTA BE CAREFUL, MY PARENTS CAN'T FIND OUT YOU'RE HERE!

HWEEK!

AND DON'T WORRY, OUR CAT, *CARTOON,* WON'T PESTER YOU ANYMORE. I GOT HIM BUSY WITH ANOTHER ANIMAL. *HEE HEE!*

LET'S SEE IF I HAVE ANY NEW COMMENTS ON MY BLOG!

?!

ZWEEE

CARTOON! WHAT ARE YOU DOING WITH THE COMPUTER MOUSE?

16

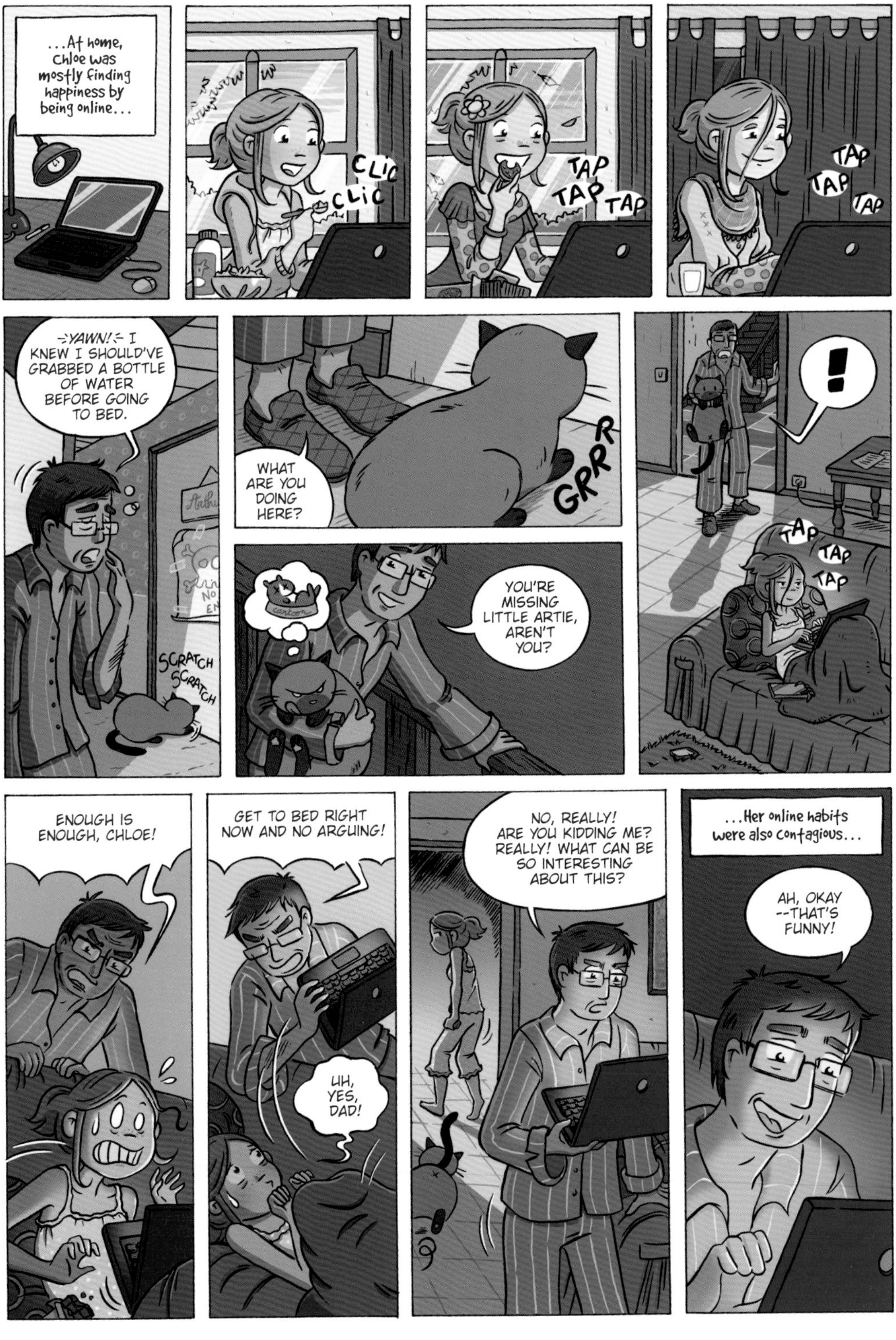

...At home, Chloe was mostly finding happiness by being online...
CLIC CLIC
TAP TAP TAP
TAP TAP TAP
-YAWN!- I KNEW I SHOULD'VE GRABBED A BOTTLE OF WATER BEFORE GOING TO BED.
SCRATCH SCRATCH
WHAT ARE YOU DOING HERE?
GRRR
YOU'RE MISSING LITTLE ARTIE, AREN'T YOU?
!
TAP TAP TAP
ENOUGH IS ENOUGH, CHLOE!
GET TO BED RIGHT NOW AND NO ARGUING!
UH, YES, DAD!
NO, REALLY! ARE YOU KIDDING ME? REALLY! WHAT CAN BE SO INTERESTING ABOUT THIS?
...Her online habits were also contagious...
AH, OKAY --THAT'S FUNNY!

From our young heroine's perspective, only her new virtual life seemed to count...

HEY, ALEX, I BEAT MY RECORD YESTERDAY WITH MY BLOG AND ITS SUPER STYLE PAGES!

TEEP

NO FEWER THAN 236 VISITORS AND 73 COMMENTS-- *OUTSTANDING!*

AWESOME!

IF YOU LIKE, NEXT WEEK WE COULD DO A SERIES OF PHOTOS OF THE TWO OF US!

MY PUBLIC WOULD LOVE IT!

SURE, WHY NOT? OKAY, I'M OUT OF HERE!

TEEP

TEEP

I DON'T RECOGNIZE OUR LITTLE MISTY THESE DAYS, TONY.

IT'S ADOLESCENCE, DEAR. IT'S NOTHING SERIO--

TEEP TEEP TEEP

TAP TAP TAP

SIGN, PLEASE!

HMM--

TAP TAP

SCRITCH

Permission Slip
I, the undersigned, Mr. or Mrs. Blin, the authorize my that son Arthur now is att first-grade.

ame: Thingamabob
ecies: Guinea pig
n duration: 3 months

Signature:

18

By chance or coincidence, 9th grade student council elections took place around that time...

WE NEED TWO REPRESENTATIVES!

FATOUMA'S ALREADY VOLUNTEERED. I KNOW IT'S IMPORTANT TO HER, AND THAT'S A GOOD THING!

I NEED SOMEONE ELSE, NONETHELESS.

FRCHH

ZZZZZ

ZZZZ

POC

YES?

AH! VERY GOOD, CHLOE! WAY TO TAKE THE INITIATIVE AT LAST. YOU'LL BE A VERY GOOD REPRESENTATIVE.

SCRITCH SCRITCH

SO, LET'S GET STARTED WITH CLASS AGAIN! AS I WAS TELLING YOU, MAHATMA GANDHI, EVEN THOUGH ADVOCATING CIVIL DISOBEDIENCE, WAS AN APOSTLE OF NON-VIOLENCE.

?

CLASS REP?

I HOPE THIS DOESN'T INVOLVE ANYTHING TOO COMPLICATED!

TEEP
TEEP

?!

I'LL BE HONEST, BEING PARTNERED WITH YOU CLEARLY WASN'T MY CHOICE--

--BUT SEEING AS HOW YOU'RE ON STUDENT COUNCIL NOW, IT'S HIGH TIME YOU STOPPED BEING SO FRIVOLOUS. YOU'LL HAVE TO LEARN TO TAKE A STAND AND FIGHT, BECAUSE NOBODY IS TAKING ACTION!

LET'S SEE WHOSE NASTY HEAD THIS HAT ENDS UP ON... HA HA HA!

MIREILLE IS A TORTURER--

--THE SCHOOL'S DEMONIC, MALEVOLENT DEAN OF DISCIPLINE!

I KNOW YOU GET ALONG WELL WITH THAT LITTLE SIXTH-GRADER, ELYSE. JUST REALIZE SHE'S ONE OF THOSE WHO'S SUFFERING THE MOST!

I HAVEN'T FOUND A WAY TO STOP MIREILLE YET, OR TO STOP ANISSA AND HER FRIENDS EITHER, BUT I WANTED YOU TO BE AWARE OF IT. IT'S UP TO YOU TO DRAW YOUR OWN CONCLUSIONS!

20

That evening at dinner, Chloe still seems out of sorts...

THAT'S WHY I NEVER SEE ELYSE ANYMORE! AND I HADN'T NOTICED A THING SINCE SCHOOL STARTED BACK UP.

DINNER IS GOING TO GET COLD.

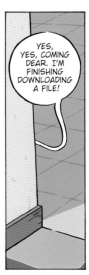

YES, YES, COMING DEAR. I'M FINISHING DOWNLOADING A FILE!

AND YOU'RE NOT EATING EITHER, MISTY!

IS IT NOT GOOD?

DON'T YOU THINK THERE ARE WORSE THINGS IN LIFE THAN NOT EATING DINNER?

OKAY, WE'LL LET THAT GO. FOR NOW. BUT ARTIE, I'VE NEVER SEEN YOU BEHAVE SO WELL AS YOU HAVE LATELY!

YOU GET DRESSED BY YOURSELF, YOU CLEAN UP YOUR ROOM, AND NOW YOU EAT ALL YOUR VEGGIES-- GOOD BOY!

YES, OF COURSE, MOMMY!

Chloe's fashion Blog

Home ♥ FAQ ♥ Lookbook ♥ Links ♥ Contact

Remember, if you want to be as photogenic as me,
your hairstyles and outfits must always match! :)

Published by Chloe at 1:20pm

50 comments   Vote for this image ✮✮✮✮☆

Laid back, chic, rock -- Nothing simpler
to get a fashion victim noticed at school!

Published by Chloe at 10:42pm

✮✮✮☆☆

The lastest phone! Ideal for communicating with
your sweetie while still looking awesome!

Published by Chloe at 10:56pm

38 comments   Vote for this image ✮✮✮☆☆

Because not everybody
has a sense of style--
This is a logbook of photos
of my coolest
outfits, inspirations,
and poses.

Chloe!

Shopping Selection

Write to me!

Mobilization

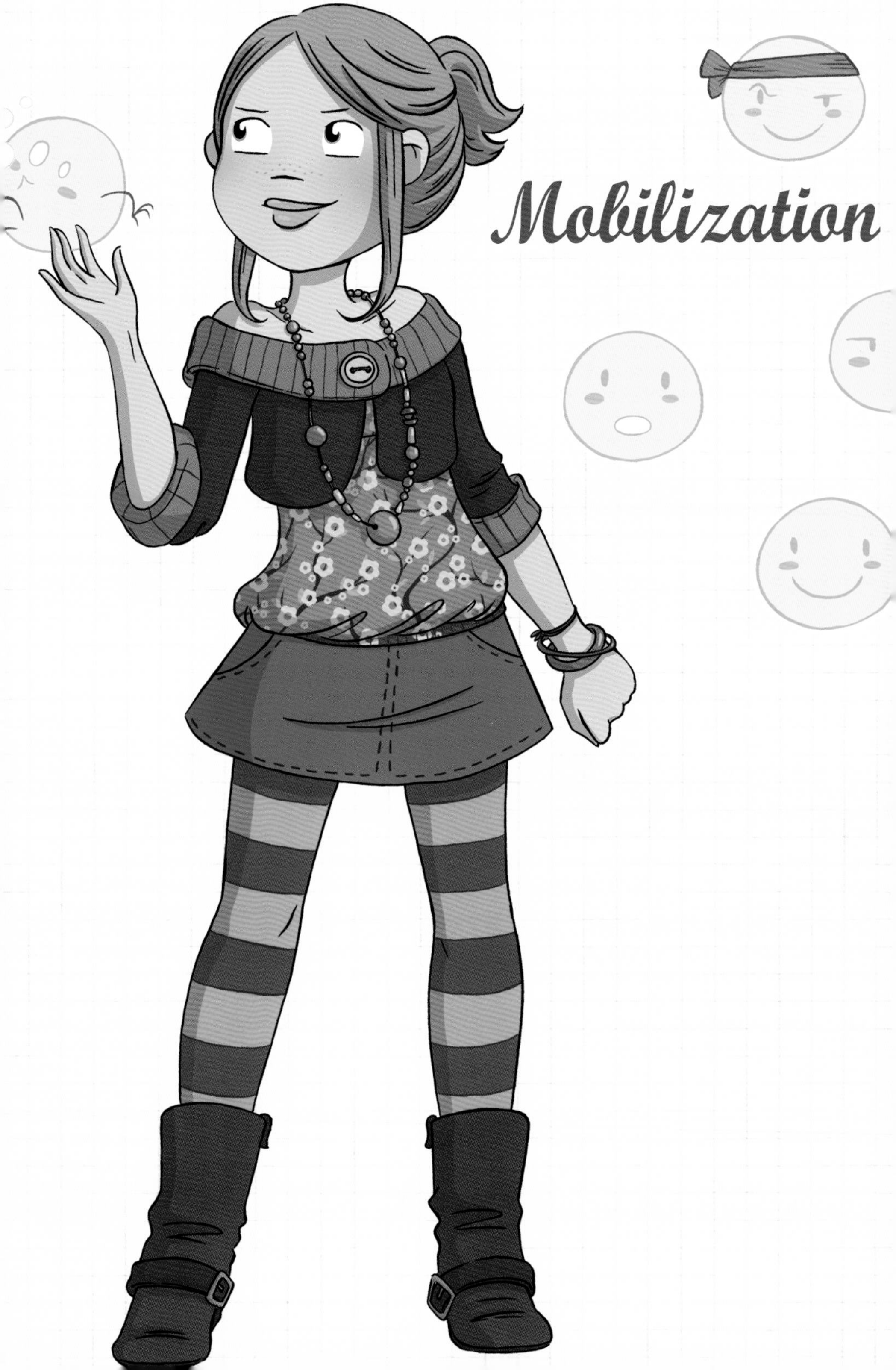

TEE BEE LEET

new message

OH, NO! ALEX IS CANCELLING ONCE AGAIN FOR THIS WEEKEND.

BEEP BEEP

THAT WAS OUR LAST CHANCE TO SEE EACH OTHER, TOO, BEFORE HE GOES AWAY ON VACATION WITH HIS PARENTS!

IT CAN'T BE!

GRRRRR

DON'T TELL ME YOU SPENT THE WHOLE NIGHT HERE. DID YOU, *TONY*?

UH-- IT'S UH-- WELL--

OKAY, NO BLOG THIS MORNING EITHER--I DON'T THINK I'M IN THE MOOD FOR IT TODAY!

I'M GOING FOR A WALK, MOM.

FINE, FINE ...UH... SEE YOU LATER, CHLOE!

AND WOULD IT BE TOO MUCH TO ASK YOU TO SIGN OFF A LITTLE, TOO, ON WEEKENDS?!

NO ANSWER FROM MARK!

TEEP TEEP

I'VE REALLY GOT TO FIND SOMEONE TO TALK TO, BUT WHO?

TEEP TEEP

CONTACTS

Papa
Parrain Etienne
Pauline
Prof of guitar

Q

R

App

TEEP TEEP TEEP

UNLESS--

I HOPE THAT, DESPITE HIS CLINGY GIRLFRIEND *DAPHNE*, MY *UNCLE STEVE* WILL HAVE SOME TIME FOR ME! I'LL TRY TO EXPLAIN EVERYTHING TO HIM--

I'M REPEATING MYSELF, BUT THANKS FOR LISTENING TO ME, UNCLE STEVE!

IT'S NO BIGGIE, CHLOE!

I GUESS I'M JUST CONFUSED.

I JUST DIDN'T KNOW HOW TO TELL ANYONE.

NO WORRIES, JUST LET YOURSELF BE SOOTHED BY THE POSITIVE WAVES, AS WE TAKE OUR TRIP!

DAPHNE'S AT A CONFERENCE TILL SUNDAY EVENING--

I CHECKED WITH YOUR FOLKS--

AND MY COMMITMENT GURU, TOO--

YOUR COMMITMENT GURU?

BRMVV
TOOF
TOOF

MISS SUZANNE, MY GODMOTHER OF COMMITMENT!

VVVVVRRBVRRRRRR

For mechanical reasons, the trip went on too long...

WWRRRRRRrrr

♪ Yellow submarine ♪ Yellow submarine ♪

...and Chloe had too much time for painful memories...

♪ Help ♪♪ ♪ I need somebody ♪ ♪ Help ♪

...Nevertheless, the chance to enjoy a few hours with her godfather warmed our young heroine's heart!

...SO, YOU SEE, THAT WOULD BE LIKE TORTURE FOR ANISSA AND HER BROOD!

IF THEY START BOTHERING YOU AGAIN, I'LL SEND THEM TO DO AN INTERNSHIP HEREABOUTS!

HEE HEE HEE!

DANG, I DON'T HAVE RECEPTION ANYMORE!

SO WHAT? LUCKY FOR US, ISN'T IT? WE GET TO ENJOY EACH OTHER'S COMPANY EVEN MORE.

YEAH, YOU'RE RIGHT, IT'S BEEN A WHILE--

Just like in a dream, moments of surprise and grace quickly followed one after the other...

STEVE, MY STUDENT OF COMMITMENT, WHAT A JOY TO SEE YOU AGAIN!

HELLO, CHLOE!

?!

THIS CROWN, YOUNG LADY, IS A SIGN OF WELCOME TO SUZANNE'S DOMAIN!

AH ...UH...OKAY... ...WELL...UH... THANKS, MISS SUZANNE!

NOT "MISS OR MISSUS" HERE, JUST CALL ME SUZY!

FOLLOW ME!

IMPRESSIVE, HUH?

THE SIXTIES AND SEVENTIES ARE VERY DEAR TO ME.

YES, I CAN TELL! HEE HEE!

HOW DID YOU MEET MY UNCLE STEVE?

AH! MEETING YOUR UNCLE!

IT WAS A GOOD FIFTEEN YEARS AGO NOW-- BUT WHAT A LOVELY ENCOUNTER!

WE WERE PROTESTING BACK THEN, NOT FAR FROM HERE, AGAINST PLANS TO BUILD AN ENORMOUS COMMERCIAL COMPLEX--

STEVE WAS VACATIONING, AND HE STUMBLED ON US BY CHANCE, AND BRAVELY JOINED US IN OUR STRUGGLE!

IS THAT TRUE, UNCLE STEVE?

OF COURSE IT'S TRUE! IT WAS MY FIRST PROTEST, TOO-- A TRUE, BEAUTIFUL CAUSE TO DEFEND AND, QUITE NATURALLY, SUZY OFFERED TO BECOME MY TEACHER!

YES! A GOOD CAUSE ALWAYS DESERVES DEFENDING. DON'T YOU THINK SO, CHLOE?

YES, OF COURSE--

SO, DINNER TIME!

I DON'T KNOW ABOUT YOU, BUT I'VE GOT A CASE OF THE MUNCHIES! HA HA HA!

NOTHING BETTER THAN GOOD, ORGANIC KEBABS, IS THERE, YOUNG LADY?

YES, THANKS, IT'S REALLY GOOD!

DON'T BE SAD, CHLOE! YOU KNOW, STEVE EXPLAINED EVERYTHING TO ME.

JUST KNOW THAT EVEN IF YOU HEAD BACK TOMORROW MORNING TO MANY MORE TESTS OF THE SPIRIT IT'S ALWAYS POSSIBLE TO GET BACK TO THE ESSENTIALS.

WE ALL MAKE MISTAKES-- REDISCOVER THE VALUES THAT ARE YOURS AND DON'T HESITATE TO TAKE ACTION IF THE CAUSE SEEMS RIGHT TO YOU. BUT, BE CAREFUL, ALWAYS STRIVE TO BE NON-VIOLENT!

NON- VIOLENT LIKE GANDHI?

YES, LIKE GANDHI, BUT ESPECIALLY LIKE SUZY!

Armed with all the advice she'd received, Chloe quickly tried to get it together...

DROP ME OFF HERE, UNCLE STEVE! DROP ME OFF HERE!

THANKS FOR AN AWESOME WEEKEND!

AND GOOD LUCK CLEANING YOUR CAR OFF! HEE HEE!

HI, *ENZO!*

OH, HI, CHLOE!

UH...SAY... YOU DON'T HAVE ANY NEWS FROM ALEX BY ANY CHANCE?

UH-- NO--

I DIDN'T SEE HIM TODAY!

WHEN YOU SEE HIM, THEN, PROMISE TO TELL HIM I THINK ABOUT HIM ALL THE TIME! OKAY?

MARK, MARK! WAIT UP!

I'VE BEEN PRETTY STUPID LATELY--

YOU THURE HAVE!

BUT I PROMISE YOU I'M DONE WITH THAT! I MISSED BEING FRIENDS-- AND I'LL MAKE IT UP TO YOU! WHAT'S MORE, I'VE GOT LOADS OF STUFF TO TELL YOU!

The following day, at school, our young heroine knew right away what to do...

FATOUMA! FATOUMA!

I THOUGHT ABOUT IT AND, FROM NOW ON, I'M TOTALLY WITH YOU!

I WANT TO KNOW EVERY-THING.

THAT'S FANTASTIC!

HERE'S SOMEONE IN REAL NEED OF BEING REASSURED ON THAT SCORE.

ELYSE, I WANTED TO TELL YOU I KNOW ABOUT THE PROBLEMS YOU AND THE OTHER SIXTH-GRADERS ARE HAVING WITH MIREILLE!

AND NOW SEVERAL OF US HERE KNOW ABOUT IT, TOO.

FATHOUMA AND CHLOE ARE CLATH REPRETHENTATITH, TOO!

HEE HEE!

Even if the game was far from being won...

WHAT'S THIS GATHERING ABOUT?

BREAK IT UP, BREAK IT UP!

I JUST HAVE A FEW MONTHS LEFT UNTIL RETIREMENT. THEY'RE NOT GONNA RUIN MY FINAL YEAR! ORDER, WE MUST HAVE ORDER!

...Chloe was better acquainted with the true depth of her adversaries' depravity.

KEEP YOUR BALANCE!

HA HA HA!

MERCY...

MERCY! HA HA HA! THAT'S A GOOD ONE!

LAST TIME SHE MADE ME DO PLANK EXERCISES FOR ALMOST A HALF-HOUR!

IT'S WORSE FOR ME, I HAD TO STAND STILL WHILE STARING AT THE WALL FOR MORE THAN AN HOUR!

WE'VE NEVER DONE ANYTHING WRONG, EITHER!

UNFORTUNATELY, THIS HAS ALSO INSPIRED OTHERS.

WHY IS MIREILLE SO INTENT ON BEING MEAN?

THAT'S STILL A MYSTERY.

In the face of this alarming observation, Chloe and Fatouma immediately tried to turn to other allies at the school...

MAYBE **JULES** COULD HELP US-- HE WORKS DIRECTLY WITH MIREILLE. HE'S A PART-TIME ASSISTANT HERE. WHAT'S MORE, HE'S REALLY NICE!

Study Hall

YES, THAT'S AN IDEA!

JULES!

OKAY ...UH...UH... KIDS, I'LL JUST BE TWO SECONDS.

WHAT IS THIS MESS?!

NICE HE MAY BE, BUT UNFORTUNATELY HE'S ALREADY UNDER HIS SUPERVISOR'S THUMB!

PRINCIPAL

AND THE PRINCIPAL?

YOU KNOW, CHLOE, FOR THE TWO YEARS SINCE HE'S BEEN HERE, VERY FEW HAVE EVER SEEN **MR. DUMONT**, AND SOME PEOPLE SAYS HE'S EVEN MORE DIABOLICAL THAN MIREILLE, WITH SCARY EYES!

PRINCIPAL

THAT'S WHAT THEY SAY, HUH? OKAY, WE'LL FORGET ABOUT HIM, THEN!

UH-- WAIT!

LIBRARY

NOK NOK

I DON'T THINK ANYONE IN THE LIBRARY CAN HELP US EITHER!

CLIC

IT LOOKS LIKE YOU'RE THINKING OF *MRS. MOLLAS*. DON'T WORRY, SHE'S CHANGED SCHOOLS! IN FACT, SHE'S BEEN REPLACED BY *MISS TILLET*. MAYBE SHE CAN HELP US.

WOW, THIS LOOKS A HECKUVA LOT BETTER ORGANIZED THAN BEFORE!

AND A LOT MORE PEOPLE!

WHAT'S WEIRD, THOUGH, IS THAT IT'S MOSTLY BOYS IN HERE!

IT'S NOT SO STRANGE AS ALL THAT. LOOK!

TAP TAP

WHO'S NEXT?

WE ARE, WE ARE!

PLEASE, BOYS, A LITTLE QUIET!

I'LL TAKE CARE OF YOU IN A MOMENT.

SO, FATOUMA, ARE YOU BRINGING ME A GREAT NEW READER?

YES, THIS IS CHLOE!

SO, WE'D ACTUALLY LIKE YOU TO HELP US FIND THE BEST INFO ON PROTESTS AND MAKING DEMANDS.

SAY, THAT'S VERY, VERY INTERESTING! WHAT'S THIS ABOUT?

IT'S ABOUT MIREI--

UH-- NO, NO, IT'S JUST FOR HISTORY CLASS!

Even though their research didn't come easily...

SO, THE NERDS ARE LOST IN THOUGHT? HEE HEE HEE!

MAYBE THEY'RE DEAF, YOU THINK?

WAK

DO YOU SEE THAT, ANISSA? THEY DIDN'T EVEN ANSWER ME!

GRRRR!

AT LEAST ONE OF THEM ISN'T BLIND, IT SEEMS!

HA HA HA!

...nevertheless, our young heroine's persistence ends up paying off!

I SHOULD HAVE THOUGHT OF THAT, FATOU!

THE INTERNET ISN'T ALL BAD!

Special Report Internet Service Info!

IF WE CAN'T SPREAD THE MESSAGE HERE, WE MUST TRY TO DO IT OUTSIDE.

AND FOR THAT, WE'LL USE MY BLOG!

WHAT'S MORE, CONSIDERING THAT THE FALL BREAK WILL BE STARTING SOON, WE'LL HAVE A LOT OF TIME TO DEVOTE TO THIS. YES!

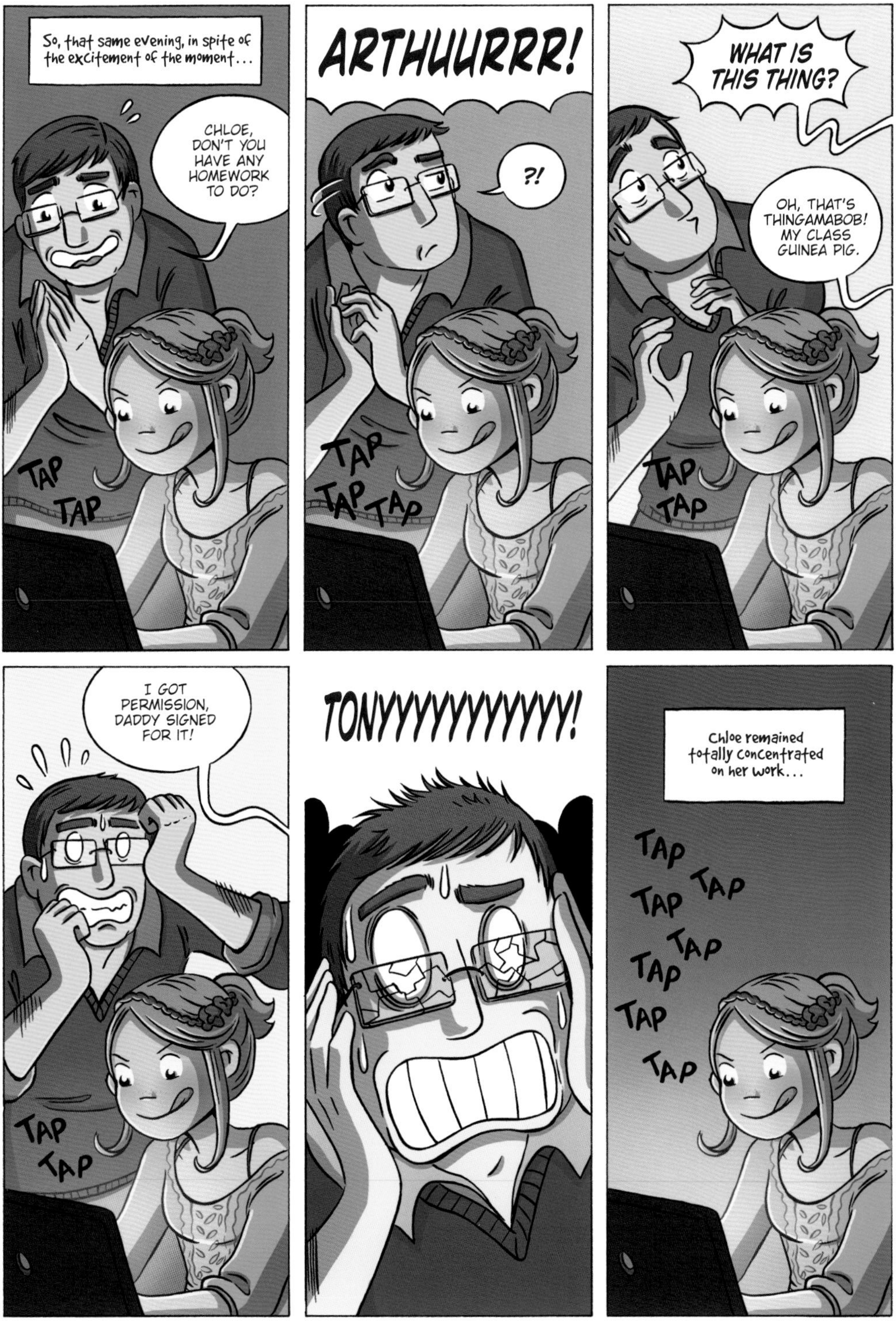
So, that same evening, in spite of the excitement of the moment...
CHLOE, DON'T YOU HAVE ANY HOMEWORK TO DO?
TAP TAP
ARTHUURRR!
?!
TAP TAP TAP
WHAT IS THIS THING?
OH, THAT'S THINGAMABOB! MY CLASS GUINEA PIG.
TAP TAP
I GOT PERMISSION, DADDY SIGNED FOR IT!
TAP TAP
TONYYYYYYYYYYY!
Chloe remained totally concentrated on her work...
TAP TAP TAP TAP TAP TAP TAP

Chloe's fashion Blog

Home ♥ FAQ ♥ Lookbook ♥ Links ♥ Contact

United, we'll fight for you!

Published by Chloe at 10:27pm.
231 comments   Vote for this image ☆ ☆ ☆ ☆ ☆

These 9th grade class reps are both stylish and committed :)

Published by Chloe at 10:42pm
112 comments   Vote for this image ☆ ☆ ☆ ☆ ☆

Open air painting -- the Suzy touch!

Published by Chloe at 10:56pm
99 comments   Vote for this image ☆ ☆ ☆ ☆ ☆

Welcome to my blog

Being stylish is one thing-- Defending good values is another. A logbook of photos-- and more-- of these new priorities.

Chloe!

Shopping Selection

Write to me!

Union

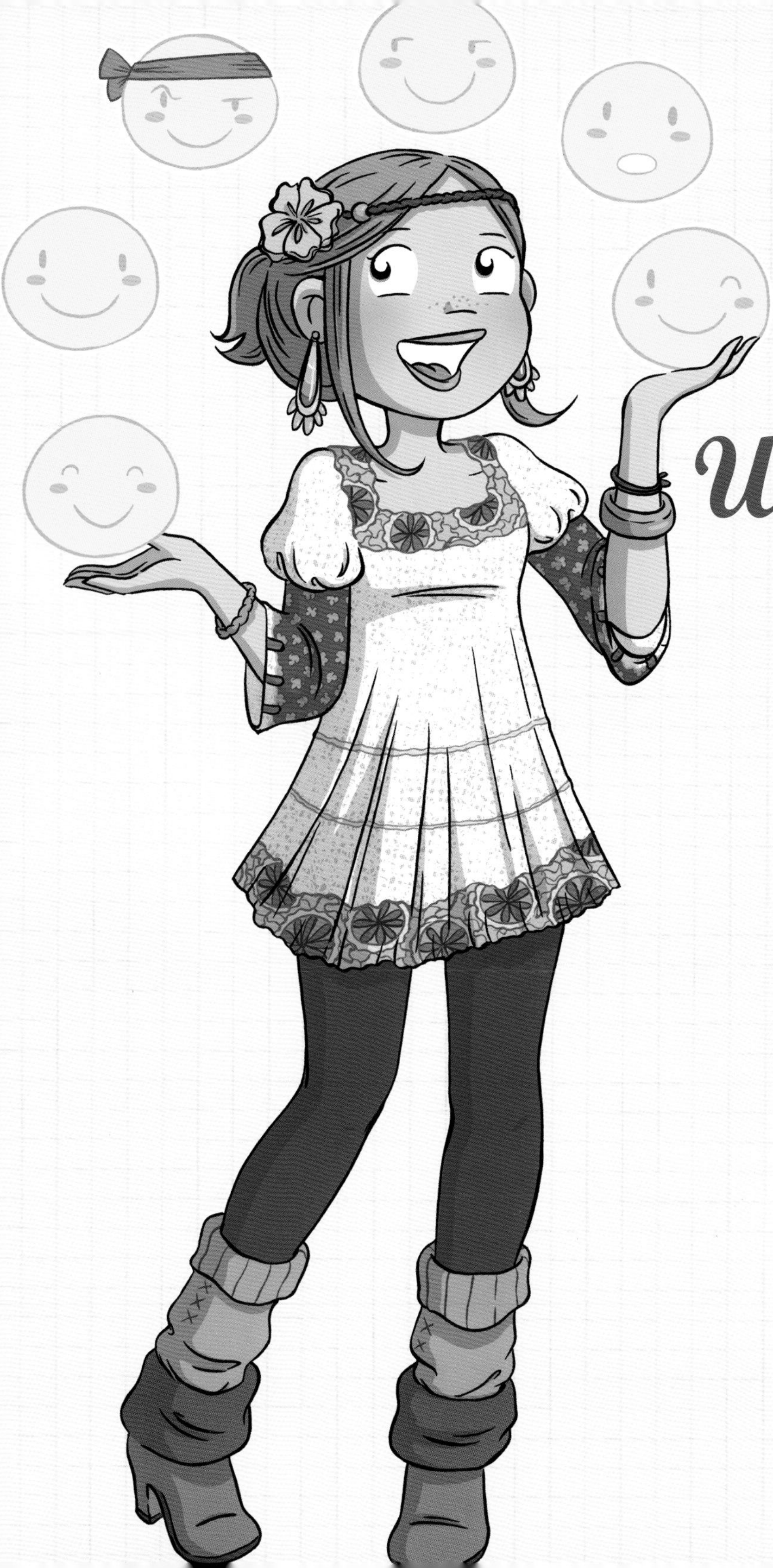

‑YAAAWN!‑ GETTING UP AT 7 A.M. DURING VACATHION! I'M TOTALLY EXTHAUTHTED!

RIIIII... THERE YOU ARE AT LAST, MARK!

I THINK WE'RE ON THE RIGHT TRACK!

HEE HEE HEE! COME IN, COME IN!

UH-- I THINK I'M MOTHTLY AWAKE, IN ANY CATHE!

HERE'S OUR LITTLE NEIGHBOR, LILOU--

MY BROTHER, ARTHUR--

HIS GUINEA PIG, THINGAMABOB--

AND OUR CAT, CARTOON!

?!

TODAY, I'M IN CHARGE OF LOOKING AFTER ALL THESE LITTLE PEOPLE!

MEOW?

OOOH! THINGAMABOB IS SO CUTE!

KWEEK!

LOOK! I'VE ALREADY GOTTEN TWO MESSAGES OF SUPPORT!

THETHE ARE PEOPLE WHO ALREADY READ YOUR BLOG, AREN'T THEY?

YES, OF COURSE! IT'S **ALICE** AND HER BROTHER, **NICO**, SOME VACATION FRIENDS. SINCE ALICE AND I ARE REALLY CLOSE, I SENT HER ALL THE INFO!

DEAL!

GOOD TEAMWORK!

YEAH, THAT'TH REALLY GREAT FOR YOUR FRIENDTH, BUT YOU THEE, IT'LL HAVE TO BE A LOT MORE PEOPLE THAT YOU DON'T KNOW!

HHHMMMMM-- THERE'TH ONLY ONE THOLUTHION LEFT! A FEW DAYTH FROM NOW, MEET AT MY HOUTH. I'LL HAVE MADE PROGRETH ON ALL THITH BY THEN!

ON THAT, TOO! HEE HEE!

BE CAREFUL! GUINEA PIGS ARE FRAGILE. YOU CAN'T JUST HOLD THEM ANY OLD WAY.

A few days later, the meeting proposed by Mark was held...

OK, WE'RE ON!

IF ELYSE HADN'T STAYED AT YOUR HOUSE, CHLOE, SHE'D HAVE REALLY BEEN IMPRESSED!

MAYBE CARTOON IS, TOO, DON'T YOU THINK?

YOU KNOW, FATOU, YOU WON'T GET MUCH OUT OF HIM TODAY! HE'S REALLY MAD BECAUSE I DIDN'T TRUST HIM ENOUGH TO LEAVE HIM ALONE WITH THINGAMABOB AND THE OTHERS AT THE HOUSE.

TADA! HERE'TH MY LATETH THET-UP--

WOOOOOOOW!

?

...with guaranteed results...

I'VE TOTALLY REVOLUTIONITHED THINGTH FOR YOU, CHLOE!

231 comments

...ished by Chloe at 10:27pm

IN FACT, JUTH AFTER HAVING OPTIMITHED THE INDECTHING REAL QUICK, YOU RETHIEVED A FEW THUPPORT METHAGETH FROM ALL OVER!

BUT ETHPETHIALLY, ETHPETHIALLY—

by Chloe at 10:27pm

Admin :

comments

new messages

CLIC

TKK TKK TKK TKK TKKTKK

GRRRRRR

ESPECIALLY WHAT? SHOW ME!

231 comments

231 Jade and Andrea, Hector Berlioz Middle School

So much unfairness is never for the best! If you want our support, we're totally in your court—

AWESOME! ANSWER THEM, THEY'RE AT A MIDDLE SCHOOL ABOUT A MILE FROM OURS!

ALREADY DONE, CHLOE! WE'RE GONNA MEET THATURDAY AT 2 O'CLOCK, AT VICTORY THQUARE.

GRRRRR

MEOW

!

BZZZ ZZZ

After that things became more efficient at home, too...

THANKS TO THIS SCHEDULE, THERE ARE TIME SLOTS TO BE USED FOR THE COMPUTER!

YOUR DAUGHTER HAS ACCEPTED THEM-- YOU SHOULD SET AN EXAMPLE, TOO, MY DEAR!

TAP TAP

AS FOR YOU, ARTIE, YOU'LL DO ME THE HONOR OF SIGNING THIS LITTLE CONTRACT I WROTE UP FOR YOU ABOUT THINGAMABOB!

THINGAMABOB CONTRACT

NO PROBLEMO, MOMMY! ELYSE HAS TAUGHT ME EVERYTHING ANYWAYS!

IT'S ABOUT TIME! I'M GLAD I WON'T HAVE ANY CONTRACTS TO WRITE UP FOR HIM.

BESIDES, CARTOON IS SUPER NICE WITH THINGAMABOB NOW!

...But there were more urgent matters for our young heroine going on...

CONFIR- MATION E-MAIL FOR JADE AND ANDREAS SENT!

CLIC

...

TAP TAP TAP

Alex

Hello

Vacation seems so long without you, Alex.
I can't wait to see you again!

Thinking about you lots, Chloe.

44

VICTORY SQUARE

ARE YOU SURE THEY CAN HELP US, CHLOE?

DON'T WORRY, ELYSE. I EXPLAINED EVERYTHING TO THEM BY E-MAIL, AND THEY REALLY SEEM SUPER COMMITTED!

IT'TH ALREADY 2:08 PM.

HEY, THAT MUST BE THEM COMING— LET'S GO MEET THEM!

HI, JADE! HI, ANDREAS! I'M CHLOE AND THIS IS--

ELYSE, I SUPPOSE!

SO YOU'RE ONE OF THE KIDS GETTING PICKED ON--

WELL, JUST KNOW, WE'RE GONNA FIX THIS!

GREAT! FOLLOW ME, THE OTHERS ARE WAITING FOR US.

WE'D ALSO LIKE TO SUPPORT ELYSE, BECAUSE WE HAVE ALSO BEEN THE VICTIMS OF INJUSTICE.

FOR ME, IT'S MY LOOK THAT CAUSED ME SOME WORRIES NOT LONG AGO.

FOR JADE, IT WAS HER PASSION FOR THE WORLD OF MANGA, BUT ESPECIALLY HER BACKGROUND THAT SOMETIMES COMPLICATED THINGS.

IT'S NOT EASY BEING ACCEPTED WHEN YOU COME FROM A DIVERSE BACKGROUND! I'VE EXPERIENCED THAT, TOO!

ON THE OTHER HAND, FOR SIXTH-GRADERS AT BRASSENS, IT'S INCOMPREHENSIBLE! MY BROTHER, FOR EXAMPLE, IS A SENIOR, BUT THAT DOESN'T MEAN HE MISTREATS ELEVENTH-GRADERS. WHAT'S MORE, USUALLY THEY LOOK OUT FOR THEM IN SOLIDARITY!

ALEX DID THAT TOO!

THAT'S TOTALLY RIGHT, FATOUMA! JADE AND I ARE MINDFUL OF THAT, TOO. SINCE WHEN SHOULD BEING IN SIXTH GRADE BE A PROBLEM?

RIGHT!

LET'S START OVER, THEN! ANDREAS AND JADE, YOU'LL START THE PREP WORK FOR BERLIOZ. MEANWHILE, WE'LL LAUNCH PHASE 1 OF THE PLAN. MY FRIENDS, WE HAVE A LOT ON OUR PLATES!

ACTHION, REACTHION!

The next day, in spite of the difficulties in middle school, the plan was set into motion...

YOU, THERE! TAKE OFF THAT HOODIE!

THERE'S NO REASON TO CARRY ON SO-- I'LL HAVE TO CALL THE PRINCIPAL!

NOOOO, NOOOOOO, PLEASE, NOT MR. DUMONT!

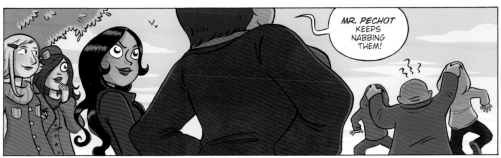

MR. PECHOT KEEPS NABBING THEM!

HA HA HA! PECHOT THE NABBER, HA HA HA!

HERE ARE YOUR INSTRUCTIONS! HANG IN THERE, LAY LOW FOR A JUST A FEW MORE DAYS.

...it was a plan that disturbed some...

Cafeteria

WHAT'S GOTTEN INTO THEM?

IT'S NOT POSSIBLE, NO JOSTLING...

HOW WILL I CATCH ONE OF THEM?! AT LEAST ONE OF THEM HAS TO MOVE!

ARGRGGHH!

WAK

I SAW YOU! IT'S USELESS TO FIGHT. ALL RIGHT, COME WITH ME, DETENTION!

OKAY, COMING, MS. MIREILLE!

MAY I COME, TOO?

OH, YES, ME, TOO!

IT'D BE SUCH A PLEASURE!

THERE'S SOMETHING REALLY FISHY ABOUT THIS!

DO YOU UNDERSTAND WHAT'S GOING ON, ANISSA?

THEY'RE NOT EVEN PROTESTING ANYMORE.

THERE, YOU SEE, AS PLANNED, OUR DIVERSION WORKED!

WE CAN DEFINITELY SAY THAT MIREILLE HAS HAD A NASTY WEEK! HEE, HEE!

SO NOW WE JUST HAVE TO GO ON TO THE NEXT PHASE!

YES, AND THERE'LL BE A FEW MORE OF US IN THIS BATTLE.

SHOW THEM, *FAUSTINE*, HOW YOUR ARTISTIC TALENTS CAN BE VALUABLE TO US!

WOW!

♥

SO NITHE!

HEE HEE! THANKS!

AND THAT'S NOT HER ONLY TALENT, BUT YOU'LL DISCOVER THAT WHEN THE TIME COMES! MEANWHILE, ON THE ROAD TO VICTO--

--RY.

I'D HAVE LOVED TO HAVE YOU CLOSE BY, ALEX! TOMORROW'S THE BIG DAY, AND I HAVEN'T SEEN YOU YET.

The time for the final confrontation had finally arrived.

JUST LIKE SUZY TOLD YOU! NON-VIOLENCE ABOVE ALL--

I PROMISE, UNCLE!

...and boy were they in for some unforgettable emotions!

WOW!

PEACE LOVE

I'M SUPER MOVED TO SEE ALL OF YOU HERE!

BUT-- WHAT-- WHAT'S THAT?!

YIPPEE! IT LOOKS LIKE FAUSTINE'S A PRO AT DOGSLEDDING, TOO!

EVEN ENZO IS HERE-- IF ONLY--

NICE INTERNET EXPLOITS, MISS CHLOE!

ALEX, AT LAST!

YOU HAVE MAJORLY IMPRESSED ME, MY LITTLE, COOL DUDE!

CHIC HIPPIE, NOT COOL DUDE! HEE HEE!

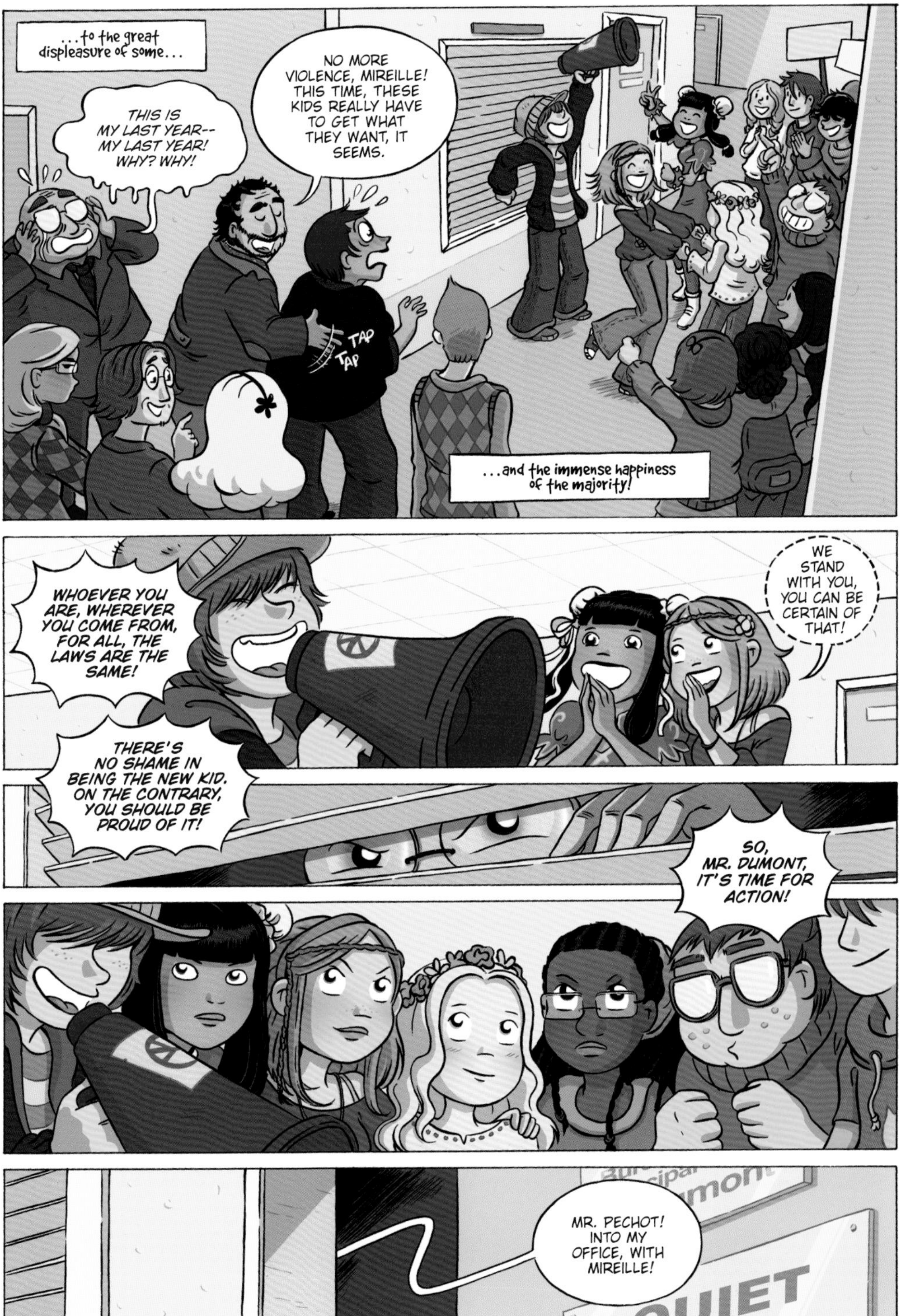
...to the great displeasure of some...
THIS IS MY LAST YEAR-- MY LAST YEAR! WHY? WHY!
NO MORE VIOLENCE, MIREILLE! THIS TIME, THESE KIDS REALLY HAVE TO GET WHAT THEY WANT, IT SEEMS.
TAP TAP
...and the immense happiness of the majority!
WHOEVER YOU ARE, WHEREVER YOU COME FROM, FOR ALL, THE LAWS ARE THE SAME!
WE STAND WITH YOU, YOU CAN BE CERTAIN OF THAT!
THERE'S NO SHAME IN BEING THE NEW KID. ON THE CONTRARY, YOU SHOULD BE PROUD OF IT!
SO, MR. DUMONT, IT'S TIME FOR ACTION!
MR. PECHOT! INTO MY OFFICE, WITH MIREILLE!
QUIET

The first questions...

IT WAS AS BAD AS THAT?

YOU SHOULD HAVE TALKED TO US!

WE REALLY DIDN'T KNOW HOW TO MAKE YOU UNDERSTAND!

THERE WAS A LOT OF PRESSURE ON US...

IT'S AWFUL!

I'VE HEARD THAT MIREILLE HAD A VERY DIFFICULT YEAR IN SIXTH GRADE, TOO.

YOU WERE VERY BRAVE IN ANY CASE!

...then a long wait followed...

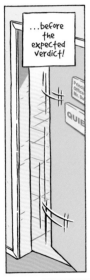

...before the expected verdict!

WELL--

MR. DUMONT LOOKS KIND OF NICE, AFTER ALL.

WHO'D HAVE THOUGHT?

OUR ROLE IS TO LET YOU MIDDLE-SCHOOLERS EXPERIENCE YOUR EDUCATION IN THE BEST CONDITIONS. EVEN IF THE METHOD WASN'T VERY CONVENTIONAL, I'D LIKE TO THANK YOU ALL, CHLOE BLIN AND FATOUMA SIMBA ESPECIALLY, AS CLASS REPRESENTATIVES, FOR BRINGING THIS INFORMATION TO MY ATTENTION.

YOU'VE JUST PERFORMED A CIVIC DUTY!

ANYTHING TO ADD, PERHAPS, MIREILLE?

I-I-I'M SORRY FOR ALL THE BAD THINGS I DID!

I COULDN'T HELP MYSELF. I JUST DID WHAT ADULTS HAVE ALWAYS DONE TO ME.

BUT NO MORE BULLYING YOU. TODAY I'LL FINALLY GET A NEW LEASE ON LIFE AND ASSERT MYSELF AS A WOMAN!

LOOKS LIKE THE TIDE'S TURNING. IT'S TIME TO KEEP A LOW PROFILE FOR A BIT, GIRLS!

DON'T TELL ME YOU THOUGHT YOU'D GET OFF THAT EASILY?!

Chloe's fashion Blog

Home ♥ FAQ ♥ Lookbook ♥ Links ♥ Contact

Always keep the best for last ;)

Posted by Chloe at 1:20pm

520 comments   Vote for this image ☆☆☆☆☆

With such stylish friends, we couldn't lose!

Posted by Chloe at 8:42pm

376 comments   Vote for this image ☆☆☆☆☆

Trips and encounters are often a source for clothing inspiration!

Posted by Chloe at 10:56pm

283 comments   Vote for this image ☆☆☆☆☆

Welcome to my blog

When style and the common good are as one--Logbook of photos--but not only--of a shared, infectious, joy.

Chloe !

Shopping Selection

Write to me!

THANKS FOR EVERYTHING, CHLOE!

IT'S OKAY, YOU REALLY DESERVED BETTER, ELYSE!

THANKS TO ALL THREE OF YOU, TOO.

GOOD JOB! AND THANKS FOR MISSING SCHOOL TO COME PLAY YOUR PART HERE!

IT TURNS OUT THE INTERNET'S AWESOME FOR MEETING STARS! HEE HEE!

ALL OF US THANK YOU FOR YOUR FASHION ADVICE! HEE HEE!

?

TEE BEE LEET

Message reçu - Alex

Are we out of here, miss?

Répondre

GLADLY, MISTER!

AH, SO, YOU'RE BACK, ALEX? FALL BREAK IS OVER AND IT'S NEARLY CHRISTMAS VACATION.

IT'S OKAY, I DON'T WANT TO KNOW-- STAY HERE AND EAT WITH US. OUR NEIGHBORS WILL BE BY SOON!

UH, WELL ...UH...

WE'LL BE HAPPY, CHLOE MOST OF ALL, TO HAVE YOU OVER TONIGHT! I'LL TAKE YOU HOME AFTERWARDS.

I'D BE GLAD TO. THANKS!

WE HAVEN'T ALL BEEN TOGETHER LIKE THIS IN A WHILE! IT'S NICE.

TELL ME ABOUT IT!

IT'S IMPORTANT TO BE ABLE TO SHARE MOMENTS IN PERSON WITHOUT A SCREEN IN THE WAY...

RIGHT, EVERY-BODY?

KZZZ

KZZZ

HWEEK!

THE END

Test: When faced with an injustice, what do you do?

1 According to you, "Equality" goes along with:

- Trying.
- Forgetting.
- Struggling

ABOVE ALL, EQUALITY MEANS SHARING.

PERSONALLY, A LITTLE KISS WOULD BE A BIG HELP FOR ME!

2 Helping one's fellow man is:

- An obligation, you can't conceive of life differently.
- A possibility, even if it's not always obvious how to achieve that.
- Pointless, there's no use bothering with all that.

THE MAIN THING IS NOT LETTING PEOPLE WALK ALL OVER YOU!

3 People could say that your personality most often is:

- Short-tempered, you get mad lightning-fast.
- Easygoing, you adapt to every situation.
- Passionate, you love things intensely.

4 To defend an idea that's important to you, you choose above all else:

- Peaceful action, an old-fashioned sit-in and we're off!
- Dialogue, you often need to be reassured about your choices before you get going.
- Strength, you're not of a very diplomatic nature.

5 As a leader, above all, you would be:

- Unifying, you take pleasure in uniting people around you.
- Authoritarian, you won't let anybody decide for you.
- Conciliatory, primarily, you privilege every individual's fulfillment.

WE CHOOSE ORIGINALITY!

I'VE BEEN RATHER NERVOUS OF LATE.

TO SAY THE LEAST!

Answers

You mostly have:

Very little injustice for you! Naturally enthusiastic and a fighter, you always make yourself confront things bravely. You also know, however, it's not easy to be heard, to defend values, in short, to assert yourself. Consequently, you often choose group consensus to come up with a way to resolve the situation. A wise decision! Often, several are stronger than one.

You mostly have:

Whatever the problems might be, if they don't concern you directly, you don't care about them. Worse, you're just waiting for one thing: you taking advantage of the situation, too! Therefore, if you don't want to be completely isolated later on, try harder to get to know the people around you. You'll find out you have lots to learn from them and that they'll be grateful to you for it.

You mostly have:

The Sixties is a period in American history that seems to have greatly inspired you. Indeed, with a cool character, you also are a fervent defender of civil rights. Incapable of acting differently. The sufferings of others are so completely intolerable to you that you cannot but act on it. As a determined pacifist, you favor dialog over violence. So that the world of tomorrow will be better than today!

ALL TOGETHER, ALL TOGETHER, YEAH, YEAH!

BEING NICE IS A JOB ALL UNTO ITSELF!

RIGHT, GIRLS?

PEACE AND LOVE, BROTHERS AND SISTERS!

THE END

Mountains and Marvels

An invigorating December morning, in front of the Blin family's home.

SCRIIICH

SCRIIICH

I-I-I CAN'T TAKE IT ANYMORE!

AGAIN!

HAVE—HAVE YOU SEEN THE TIME, DAD? I HA-HA-HATE THE COLD, TOO!

DON'T STRESS, CHLOE. I WOULDN'T WANT YOU TO BE LATE FOR SCHOOL TODAY.

AGAIN, AGAIN!

THIS'LL BE A BIG DAY FOR YOU, SWEETIE!

HUH?!

SCRAACH SCRAACH

VRR VRRR VROOOM

A BIG DAY?

OH, CHLOE! THERE YOU ARE.

?

WE HAVE TO GET GOING. SEEMS WE'RE ON THE LIST OF NINTH-GRADERS THE PRINCIPAL WANTS TO SEE RIGHT AWAY IN THE SCHOOLYARD.

WHY ARE YOU WALKING LIKE THAT, MARK?

'CAUTH ITH THLIPPERY, FATOU!

MY DEAR STUDENTS, A GREAT PASSION HAS BEEN BORN BETWEEN THE MOUNTAINS AND OUR MIDDLE SCHOOLS. A REAL ROMANCE...

HEY, WE NEVER NOTICED! HEE HEE HEE!

EVEN THOUGH YOUR ASSESSMENT TESTING IS YOUR PRIORITY THIS YEAR, WE NOTICED MANY OF YOU DIDN'T HAVE THE CHANCE TO GO ON LAST YEAR'S SCHOOL TRIP.

THAT'S WHY, DURING THE SECOND WEEK OF CHRISTMAS VACATION, THE PTA IS PROPOSING SOMETHING SPECIAL FOR YOU--

OH, NO, ANYTHING BUT THAT!

THIS!

AWESOME!

WOW!

WICKED!

SKI TRIP

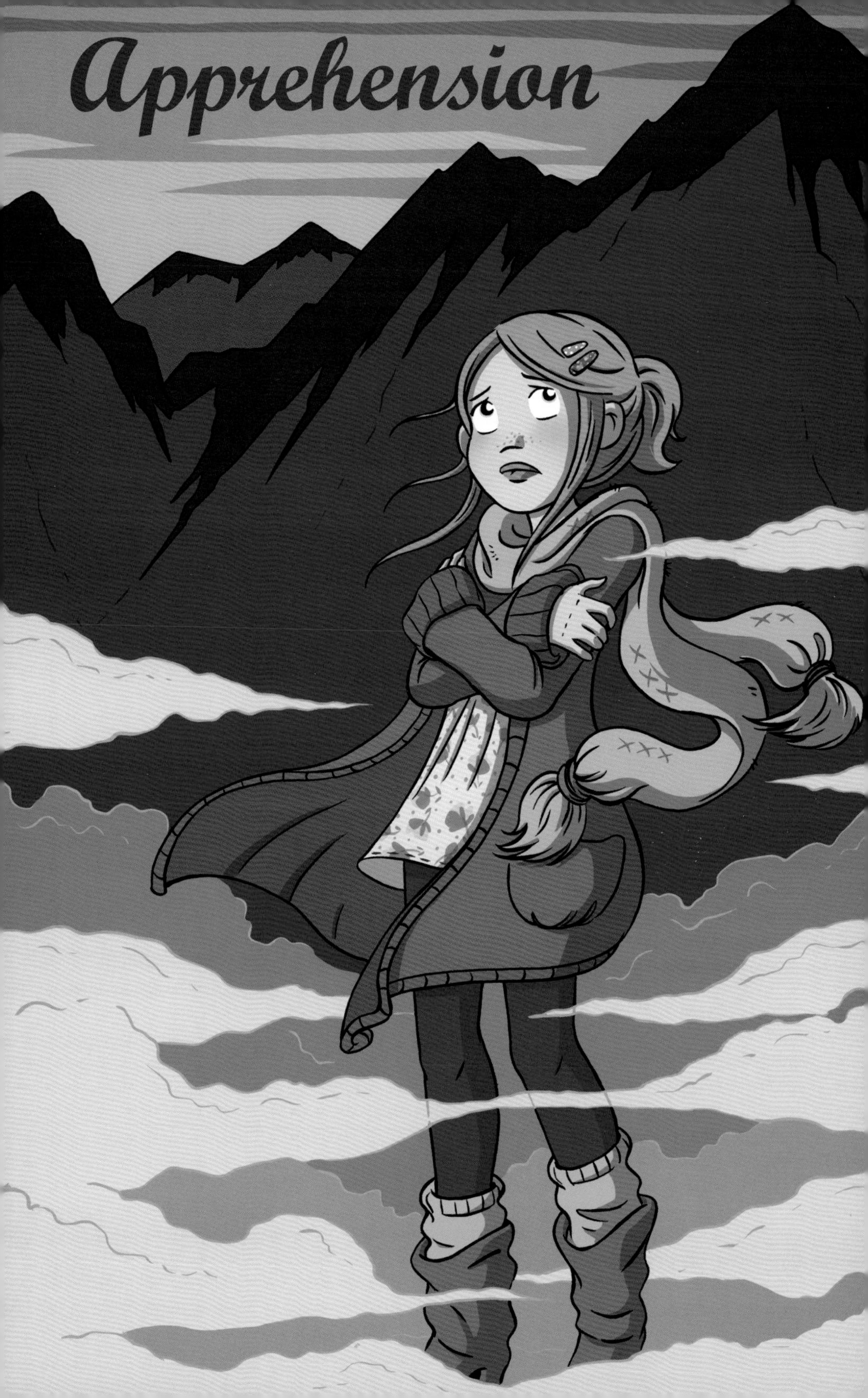
Apprehension

SO, HAPPY, KIDS?

YEEEAAAHHH!

OH, ME, TOO!

I'M HAPPY I'LL BE GOING WITH YOU.

YOU SEE, MY PARENTS HAVE MENTIONED THERE'S A SURPRISE FOR ME-- I'M SURE IT'LL BE IN THE ALPS!

IT'S SO CLASSY UP THERE, WITH STORES AND HANDSOME GUYS EVERYWHERE. HEE HEE!

YOU'LL SEE, THERE'S NOTHING BETTER THAN A LITTLE TRIP TO THE MOUNTAINS TO GIVE YOUR LEGS A STRETCH!

TO THE MOUNTAINS?

TO GIVE OUR LEGS A STRETCH?

HA HA! IT WAS A CLOSELY KEPT SECRET, WASN'T IT?

9TH GRADE SKI TRIP

FOR THE LUCKY ONES WHO'VE ALREADY BEEN NOTIFIED, YOU'RE AUTOMATICALLY PART OF THE TRIP. FOR THE OTHERS, HURRY, YOU STILL HAVE A FEW DAYS LEFT TO SEE TO THE NECESSARY STEPS!

HOWEVER, IT'S GOING TO BE TOUGH.

YOU'RE GOING TO DISCOVER A REGION WHERE THE HARSH CLIMATE AND REMOTENESS CAN REALLY HIT YOU.

YIKES!

SO, YOU'LL DIVIDE YOUR TIME BETWEEN GUIDED TOURS AND SKIING, BUT YOU'LL ALSO SAMPLE A LITTLE OF THE HISTORY OF OLDER TIMES!

SPEAKING OF WHICH, I'LL ALSO TEACH YOU A FEW WORDS OF THE LOCAL DIALECT.

After that, the coming trip was the subject of all conversations.

JULES, AS PLANNED, I'M ASSIGNING YOU TO BE THE MAIN COORDINATOR DURING THIS FIELD TRIP.

MIREILLE WON'T BE IN CHARGE THIS TIME.

TO THE MOUNTAINS?

YOU WANT US TO GO SIGN UP FOR THAT?

TOO BAD, MY PARENTS DIDN'T TELL ME ABOUT IT.

MINE EITHER-- LUCKILY! THE COLD AND COUNTRYSIDE AREN'T REALLY MY THING! HA HA HA!

YOU'LL HAVE A LOT OF RESPONSIBILITY. DON'T LET ME DOWN!

UH, OF COURSE NOT, MR. DUMONT!

SURELY YOU DIDN'T THINK I'D GO THERE ALL BY MYSELF, MY DARLING FRIENDS!

I CAN'T BELIEVE WE'RE ALREADY SIGNED UP...

IS THAT ANY REASON TO BE POUTING, CHLOE? I DON'T GET IT, IT'LL BE FUN! YOU DON'T KNOW HOW LUCKY YOU ARE TO ALREADY BE SIGNED UP.

IF YOU ONLY KNEW, FATOU.

KNEW WHAT? TELL ME!

I HATE THE COLD. I'LL BE THE ONLY ONE WHO DOESN'T KNOW HOW TO SKI. ALEX WILL BE FAR AWAY FROM ME AGAIN--

AND YOU THINK MY PARENTS ASKED WHAT I WANTED? NO!

HUH? WHAT'TH WRONG?

Even if things needed to be resolved...

THEY HAVE NO RIGHT TO MAKE ME GO ON THIS TRIP! IF I DON'T WANT TO GO, I WON'T GO!

...it definitely didn't turn out like our young heroine had imagined...

HELLO TO MY LITTLE MOUNTAIN-GIRL!

HA HA HA! DIDN'T YOUR DAD PROMISE YOU AN AWESOME SURPRISE?

LOOK, WE'VE FINISHED DECORATING THE TREE!

UH-- YES! WEREN'T YOU GOING TO FINISH LATER TODAY?

YES, YES! BUT I TOOK OFF EARLY FROM WORK TO WELCOME MY LITTLE MISTY WHO, LIKE HER DAD BACK IN HIS OWN DAY, WILL SOON BE GOING ON HER FIRST REAL SCHOOL TRIP LIKE A BIG GIRL.

I'M PROUD OF YOU, HONEY!

YOU'RE SO LUCKY! BRING ME BACK SOME SOUVENIRS, OKAY?

PSCHH

AND SOME REAL SNOW!

OH, NO! IT JUST GETS WORSE AND WORSE...

OKAY... UH... I HAVE HOMEWORK!

Fortunately, Chloe could rely on the help of her closest friends...

I'LL MISS YOU A LOT FOR THOSE FEW DAYS, CHLOE.

SO WE'LL TRY TO SPEND TONS OF TIME TOGETHER BEFORE YOU GO, OKAY?

YES!

I REALLY WISH I COULD'VE GONE SKIING WITH YOU. IT WON'T BE EASY STAYING BEHIND! THERE IS SOMETHING, HOWEVER, WE COULD DO THAT'LL HELP YOU FEEL MORE COMFORTABLE ON THE SLOPES.

REALLY? WHAT'S THAT?

THE SKATING RINK!

HELLO! WE WERE WAITING ON YOU TO PRACTICE. WE'LL BE GOING ON THE TRIP, TOO, WON'T WE, MARK?

IT WATHN'T COMPLETELY MY CHOITH, BUT WE'RE COMING, YETH.

THEY WERE BOTH WORRIED ABOUT YOU!

OHH--

THANK YOU SO MUCH!

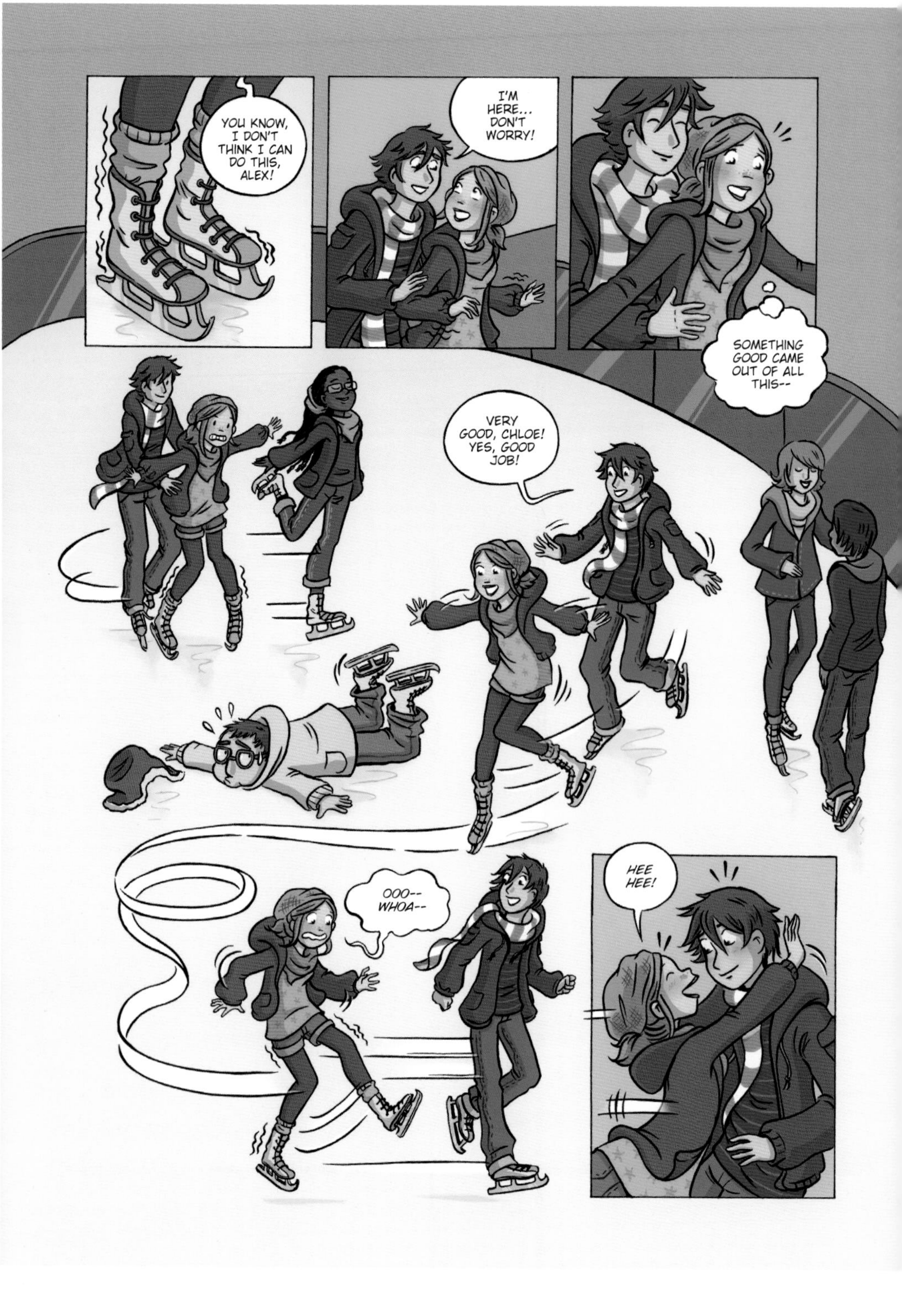
YOU KNOW, I DON'T THINK I CAN DO THIS, ALEX!
I'M HERE... DON'T WORRY!
SOMETHING GOOD CAME OUT OF ALL THIS--
VERY GOOD, CHLOE! YES, GOOD JOB!
OOO-- WHOA--
HEE HEE!

Now that the sport side of things was underway, our young heroine bravely made the best of it in the following days...

SPLOF

WITH WHAT I'M MAKING FOR YOU, YOU'LL UNDOUBTEDLY MAKE PEOPLE JEALOUS, HONEY.

I BET YOU'LL BE THE ONE WHO SELLS THE MOST CAKES DURING THE FUNDRAISER FOR THE BRASSENS MIDDLE SCHOOL SKI TRIP!

HEY! WHAT'S ALL THIS MESS?!

HEE, HEE! DADDY'S GONNA CATCH IT!

UH-- READY FOR A LITTLE TASTE TEST?

OUT! OUT! LET'S STOP THIS DISASTER!

WE'LL MAKE THIS RIGHT, CHLOE. EVERYTHING WILL BE PERFECT FOR TOMORROW, CROSS MY HEART!

PTA Cake Sale For the 9th Grade Ski Trip

9th Graders Ski Trip

MMMM-- DELICIOUS! UNIQUE! SO SWEET!

I'M TIRED OF THIS. COME ON, GIRLS!

OOPS!

OH, MY, I'M SO CLUMSY! THAT'S SO ME.

GRRR-- JUST YOU WAIT.

FORGET ABOUT IT, FATOU. IT CAN HAPPEN TO ANYONE. LUCKILY, I HAVE A CAKE LEFT THAT MY DAD MADE.

WOULD YOU LIKE A TASTE, EVEN IT'S PROBABLY NOT AS GOOD AS YOURS?

RIGHT! LET'S SEE!

YUCK-- WHAT IS THIS?

YOU'LL SEE, MR. DUMONT, THEY'RE DELICIOUS!

She had to, however, endure even more fashion self-sacrifice...

NOW YOU JUST HAVE TO TRY ON MY OUTFIT, AS WELL AS THOSE THAT LILOU'S MOM AND YOUR GODFATHER'S FIANCÉE KINDLY LOANED TO US.

OKAY, OKAY, MY LITTLE MISTY!

...for often very mixed results!

YEAH, NICE, YOU LOOK LIKE ME AT YOUR AGE!

I THINK MY MOMMY WORE THAT WHEN SHE WAS A LITTLE KID!

HA HA! JUST AS FLASHY AS WHEN I WORE IT IN THE 80'S. AT LEAST THEY'LL SEE YOU FROM A LONG WAYS OFF WITH THIS ONE!

YEP-- MIGHTY SPECIAL, ALRIGHT!

WITH ALL DUE RESPECT, SWEETIE--

BESIDES LOOKING RIDICULOUS SKIING, WHY DO I ALSO HAVE TO BE RIDICULOUS WITH MY CLOTHES? IT'S SO UNFAIR.

NOK NOK

HMMM--

THEY MADE YOU TRY THIS ON?

YES! AND OTHERS, TOO--

WELL! YOU'RE COMING SHOPPING WITH ME. MY DAUGHTER HAS TO HAVE THE BEST-- YOU CAN CHOOSE THE OUTFIT THAT YOU WANT.

THE OLD SKIER

UNCLE STEVE'S GIRLFRIEND WOULD LIKE THIS FOR SURE!

THIS WOULD BE PERFECT FOR DAD!

THAT'S MY PRINCESS, NOW!

So Christmas day finally came along...

CHLOE, IT'S TIME TO GET UP!

...with, happily, its share of memorable surprises...

I THINK SANTA CLAUS HAS BEEN BY--

QUICK, QUICK!

HE ATE EVERYTHING I LEFT FOR HIM, TOO!

~BURP!~

SHIP'S WARP DRIVES ACTIVATED! FEEOOO!

WOW!

THANKS FOR THE SCARF, THE CAP-- BUT ESPECIALLY FOR THE AWESOME SWEATER DRESS!

I REALLY LIKE IT. IT'S LIKE IT WAS HAND-KNITTED. SANTA CLAUS IS REALLY, REALLY SMART!

BY THE WAY, MY LITTLE MISTY...

SEEING AS HOW THE SCHOOL'S GOING TO ASSIGN YOU TO JOT DOWN WHAT YOU DO DURING YOUR TRIP...

I HAVE THE IMMENSE PLEASURE OF PASSING ALONG TO YOU MY SPECIAL TRAILBLAZER'S JOURNAL.

IT WENT ALONG WITH ME, IT'LL GO ALONG YOU!

The Christmas break was a short one, unfortunately. The fateful day of departure had come...

SHHHH! CAN'T YOU SEE CHLOE'S WITH HER BOYFRIEND?

DO I HAVE TO EXPLAIN EVERYTHING TO YOU TWO OR WHAT? ESPECIALLY YOU, TONY, COME ON!

DON'T FORGET, BE STRONG! YOU'VE BECOME A TRUE QUEEN OF SKATING, THAT'S NO SMALL ACHIEVEMENT.

YES, WELL, I'M STILL NOT SURE OF MYSELF.

BUT I'LL TRY, I PROMISE YOU THAT!

HERE'S A LITTLE PRESENT TO ENCOURAGE YOU, IN ANY CASE.

I TRIED TO STICK WITH THE THEME...

IT'S SO LOVELY!

I'LL COME WITH YOU!

I THINK I HAVE TO GET GOING, ALEX.

I'M HERVÉ CAMPION, YOUR DRIVER. AND WE'RE OFF!

WELCOME, EVERYONE--

UMM-- UMMM-- *NOW* WE'RE OFF!

HAIL TO THE BUS DRIVER, BUS DRIVER, BUS DRIVER,

BUS DRIVER MAN--

HE SCREAMS AND HE CUSSES, HE RAMS OTHER BUSES--

KEEP YOUR SPIRITS UP!

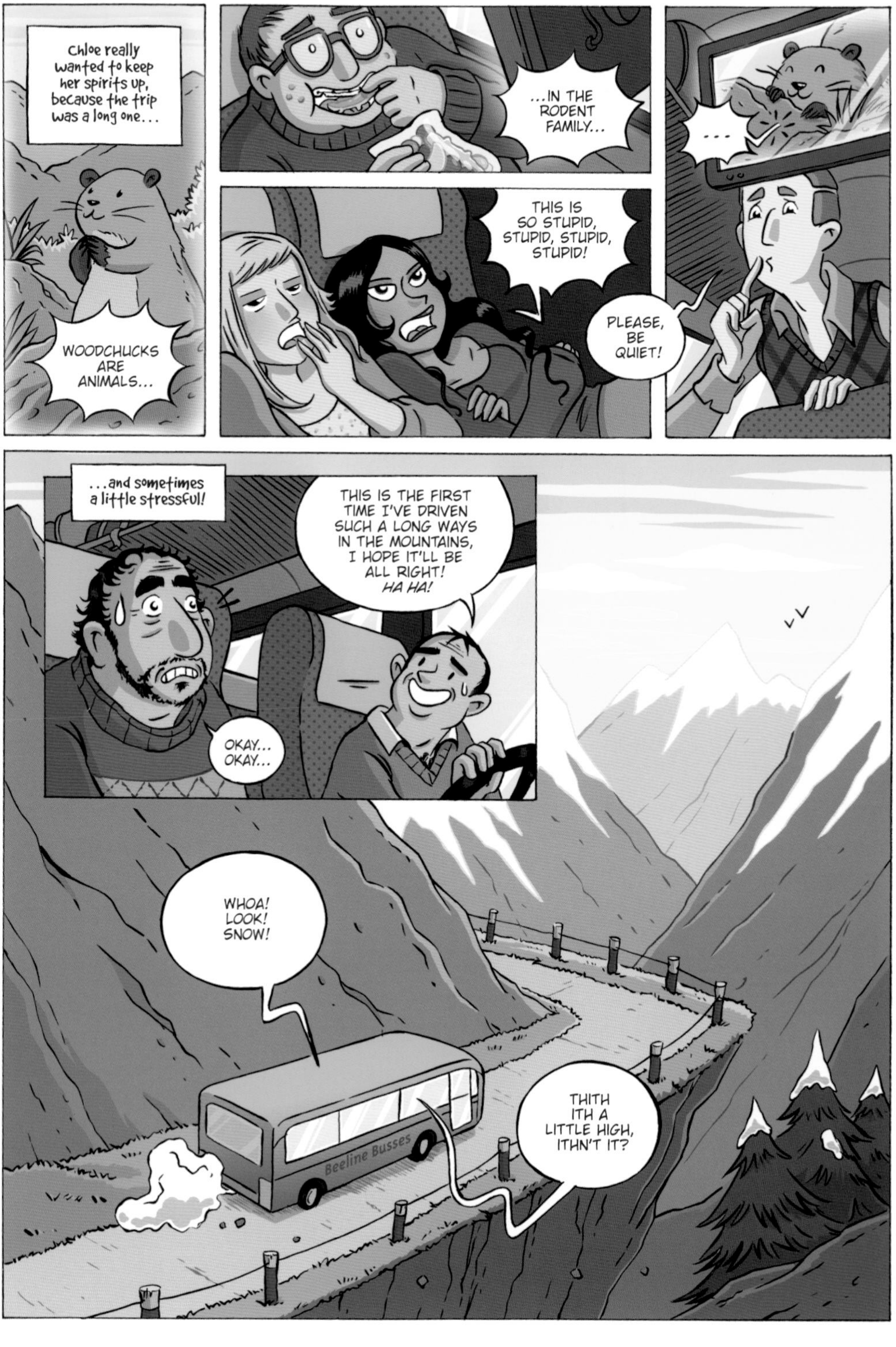
Chloe really wanted to keep her spirits up, because the trip was a long one...
WOODCHUCKS ARE ANIMALS...
...IN THE RODENT FAMILY...
...
THIS IS SO STUPID, STUPID, STUPID, STUPID!
PLEASE, BE QUIET!
...and sometimes a little stressful!
THIS IS THE FIRST TIME I'VE DRIVEN SUCH A LONG WAYS IN THE MOUNTAINS, I HOPE IT'LL BE ALL RIGHT! HA HA!
OKAY... OKAY...
WHOA! LOOK! SNOW!
Beeline Busses
THITH ITH A LITTLE HIGH, ITHN'T IT?

As for their arrival, it was marked with its own bit of unpleasantness...

BRRR-- IT'S NOT HOT AROUND HERE!

SO, HERE'S THE SCHOOL THAT'S WELCOMING US AND WHERE WE'LL SLEEP AND LIVE DURING OUR STAY. THE SCHOOL KIDS HERE ARE ON VACATION, TOO, SO WE CAN STAY IN THEIR BOARDING HOUSE.

YEAH, THIS SUCKS!

LOOK OUT!

?

WHO-- WHO DID THAT?

Poe

ARE YOU OKAY, MARK?

HEE HEE HEE!

~PFFFT~ STUPID TOURISTS!

DANG, IT WAS SOME OF THE LOCAL KIDS. IT'S TOO BAD I DON'T REMEMBER THAT LOCAL SLANG THAT MR. COSTA TAUGHT US, WE COULD'VE TALKED TO THEM!

IF WE SEE THEM AGAIN, WE'LL SAY HELLO!

Bop

TELL ME YOU'RE NOT GOING TO START BEING LIKE ANISSA, CHLOE. THIS IS PART OF OUR COUNTRY! THEY SPEAK THE SAME LANGUAGE WE DO...

TRAVEL JOURNAL

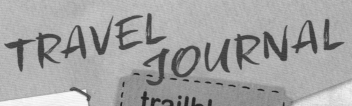

trailblazer special

by Chloe

BRRRR!
Not very reassuring, all that cold! I shiver just thinking about it...

What does your new destination look like?

Pick out the outfit you must wear to survive in this hostile environment:

danger →

What a pain!

None of those three, that's for sure!

SKATING TICKET
146016

What a horrible moment...

Are there any local expressions that you already know?

Stupid dialect! I don't ever want to hear it spoken again.

DVD: "Crazy Woodchucks"

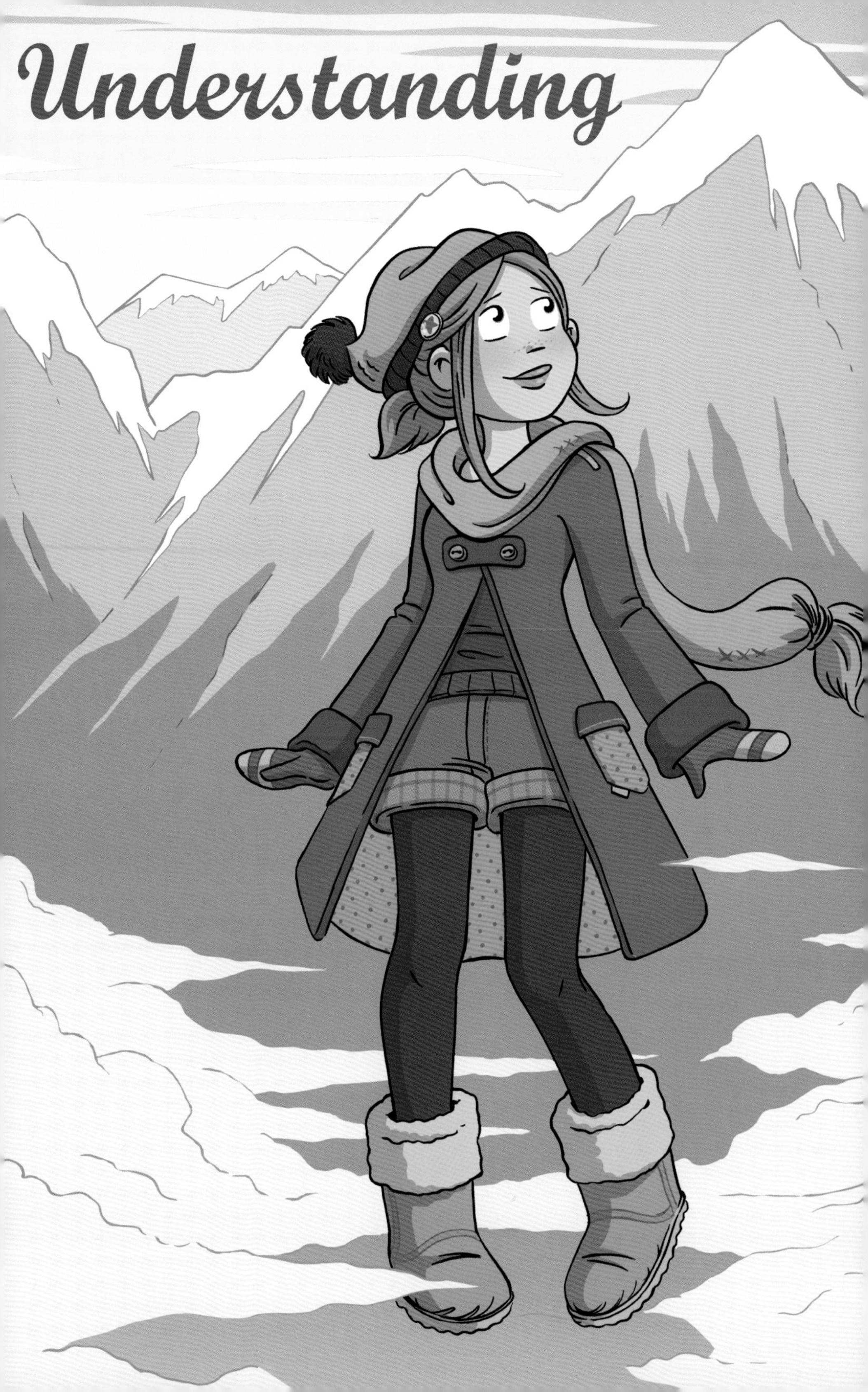
Understanding

STO-O-O-OP!

ENOUGH OF THIS RACKET! I'VE ALREADY TOLD YOU IT'D BE TWO PEOPLE TO A ROOM!

GET TO BED AND NO ARGUING!

SO, DID YOU REACH YOUR PARENTS ON THE PAYPHONE? IT'S CRAZY HOW THERE'S NO RECEPTION UP HERE!

YES, I DID. I PAID WITH COINS!

I HAD TO WAIT FOR *MISS VERNIER* TO GET DONE AND I USED UP ALL MY CHANGE, BUT THAT'S OKAY. I TALKED TO MY PARENTS, MY UNCLE, AND ALEX, TOO!

NOW WE JUST HAVE TO BE POSITIVE, DON'T WE, SINCE WE'RE HERE ANYWAYS.

I'M GLAD TO SEE YOU LIKE THIS, CHLOE!

THIS IS UNBELIEVABLE. YOU'RE DELIBERATELY DOING THAT!

QUIET!

YOU'RE RIGHT, FATOU...

ON THE OTHER HAND, WE PROBABLY WON'T HAVE THE BEST NIGHT OF OUR LIVES!

Even if everyone was frazzled from that first night, their tour was definitely getting interesting...

WELL! IT SEEMS THE MOUNTAIN AIR HASN'T HAD THE DESIRED EFFECT ON YOU YET, I SEE! HEE HEE!

I'M MR. COSTA, A HISTORY TEACHER AND CHAPERONE! TO WHOM--UM-- DO I HAVE THE PLEASURE?

I'M--

THIS IS *CLAIRE MERCIER*, THE GUIDE WHO'LL ACCOMPANY US THESE NEXT FEW DAYS.

CLAIRE, I'M JULES. WE SPOKE ON THE PHONE LAST WEEK...

YOU REMEMBER, I'M IN CHARGE OF THE GROUP!

OH, OKAY! PLEASED TO MEET ALL OF YOU--

WE START BRIGHT AND EARLY. SO, LET'S MEET IN FIVE MINUTES AT THE BUS FOR THE FIRST TOUR.

HEE HEE

HEE HEE

HEE HEE HEE

YOUR MICROPHONE, SWEET CLAIRE!

THAT'S GOOD, THAT'S GOOD, THANKS...

SO, IS THIS CUTE LITTLE MIC NOT WORKING?

TAP TAP

...

WWEEEEEEEEEE

UMM, SORRY, LITTLE DIFFICULT GETTING IT ON.

LET'S BEGIN... FIRST OF ALL, WELCOME TO OUR LOVELY REGION.

FOR TODAY, WE'RE GOING TO GO TO THE SITE OF AN ANCIENT VOLCANO.

÷YAWWWN÷ AWESOME! IS THERE NOTHING MORE MODERN AROUND THAN VOLCANOS?

THERE'RE PROBABLY MORE INTERESTING ATTRACTIONS, JUST WAIT!

THIS GUIDE SEEMS PRETTY COOL! I CAN'T WAIT TO FIND OUT MORE!

LOOK CLOSELY!

THE HILLS OR PEAKS ALL AROUND YOU ARE THE LIVING PROOF OF THE MIRACLE THAT GAVE BIRTH TO THEM.

?

?

"IT'S A PEAK, WHAT AM I SAYING, A PENINSULA!" HA HA!

NICE CYRANO REFERENCE, YOUNG LADY!

LET'S GO!

"NICE LITERARY REFERENCE"? WHY ARE YOU ACTING LIKE A NERD, LESLIE?

UH, NO! WAIT, ANISSA-- UH--

I'M NOT LIKE THAT, YOU KNOW. I'M NO SUCK-UP LIKE FATOUMA! IN FACT, I THINK I REMEMBER HEARING IT-- UM-- IN THE MUSICAL "IN LOVE WITH CYRANO"--

CAREFUL, IT'S SLIPPERY, HONEY!

YEAH-- CAREFUL! PEOPLE SEEM A BIT NUTTY AROUND HERE--

SO CAREFUL!

NO WAY, NOBODY'S NUTTY AROUND HERE.

While the walk was exhausting for some...

ARE WE THERE YET?

A MILE AND A HALF ON FOOT ~HUFF~ ~PUFF~ ~PUFF~

NEVER AGAIN!

...it also brought people together...

BEEP BEEP

IT REALLY IS BEAUTIFUL! ISN'T IT, MISS VERDIER?

CERTAINLY, EVEN IF YOU DO FEEL TOTALLY ALONE HERE, YOU KNOW.

BEEP

IT'S SO DESERTED...

YES, BUT SOLITUDE CAN OFTEN HELP US COME CLOSER TO OUR TRUE VALUES.

IT'S GREAT FOR REFLECTING.

HMMM...

LET'S CONTINUE THIS TOUR, YOU'LL SEE. IT'LL DO US ALL A WORLD OF GOOD!

HEY! WAIT UP! I FEEL LONELY, TOO! WAIT UP!

HERE WE ARE!

THIS MOUNTAIN RANGE WAS FORMED 500 MILLION YEARS AGO DURING THE PALEOZOIC ERA...

FOR THE MOST PART, THE VOLCANIC AREAS, ESPECIALLY THE LIMESTONE PLATEAUS, ARE MORE RECENT.

BLATHERING ON, SO INTERESTING, HA HA HA!

THERE'S EVERY KIND OF VOLCANO IN THIS REGION, BUT--

FFFSSHHHSH

AS YOU CAN SEE, THE CLIMATE HERE IS SOMETIMES VERY UNPREDICTABLE-- KEEP CALM, PLEASE!

SHHH

THAT BITING WIND IS CALLED THE "ÉCIR."

SSHHHSHHH

ARE "ÉCIR" INS?

FFSH

I SEE SOME OF YOU ARE STARTING TO GET TOO COLD!

SO WE DON'T END UP FROZEN, WE'LL HEAD BACK. I'LL EXPLAIN THE NEXT PART ON THE RETURN TRIP.

GOODBYE, EVERYONE! GO GET WARM!

GO IN QUIETLY.

CHLOE, ISN'T IT? I SAW EARLIER THAT YOU'D DOUBLED UP YOUR SOCKS. BE CAREFUL, YOUR FOOT'S COMPRESSED AND IT PREVENTS YOUR BLOOD FROM CIRCULATING FREELY. YOUR FEET GET COLDER!

THANKS FOR THE ADVICE!

OKAY, GOODNIGHT!

LOOK!

I'M GOING INSIDE!

DON'T BE OBSTINATE, MARK. COME WITH US!

BAM

LET'S TRY NOT TO BE SHY! THOSE THREE KIDS SEEM LIKE US, DON'T THEY, FATOU?

LET'S GO!

YEAH, IF YOU THAY THOUGH!

The time had come to redeem themselves...

UH... HI!

?

WE SAW YOU YESTERDAY AND WOULD LIKE TO GET TO KNOW YOU A LITTLE BETTER!

I HOPE YOU DON'T THPEAK IN DIALECT, HOWEVER! OUR GUIDE DOESN'T.

I LISHP A LITTLE, THASH ALL!

HER PRONUNCIATION IS COMMON IN OUR AREA, BUT THE DIALECT'S FOR OLD FOLKS! NONE OF US SPEAK IT.

BY THE WAY, I'M *ROMAIN*, AND HERE'S MY BROTHER *FLORIAN*. IF YOU CAN'T TELL AT FIRST GLANCE, WE'RE TWINS, AND OUR LISPER IS *PASCALINE*.

PLEASED TO MEET YOU! I'M CHLOE, AND THIS IS FATOUMA AND MARK!

OKAY, OKAY, WE'RE GOING.

MY BROTHER ISN'T VERY TALKATIVE, BUT UNFORTUNATELY WE CAN'T HANG OUT. WE'RE EXPECTED AT HOME.

WE'LL COME BY AGAIN TOMORROW AROUND THE SAME TIME!

LATER!

BYE.

SEE YOU TOMORROW!

The next day, the young and not so young met Claire for yet another enlightening tour...

YOU MISS ONE PERSON, THEN EVERYTHING SEEMS EMPTY, DOESN'T IT, MISS VERNIER? ESPECIALLY WHEN IT'S YOUR OTHER HALF.

UH-- YES, INDEED! HOW DID YOU KNOW?

A LITTLE BIRDY TOLD ME SO! BUT LOOK AROUND AND FORGET ALL THAT FOR A BIT...

IN THIS LAND OF GENESIS, FIRE SOMETIMES GIVES WAY TO FRESH WATER. LIKE YOUR THOUGHTS.

SO, GIVE YOURSELF THE CHANCE TO WASH AWAY YOUR PROBLEM FOR A LITTLE WHILE, CONTEMPLATING THIS MAGNIFICENT PLACE!

YOU SEEM LOST IN THOUGHT, TOO, CHLOE! ARE YOU MISSING YOUR SWEETHEART?

YES, BIG TIME!

YOU KNOW, IT WAS A ROMANTIC DISAPPOINTMENT THAT MADE ME LOVE THIS REGION. EVEN IF HIS ABSENCE IS WEIGHING ON YOU, WHAT YOU'LL EXPERIENCE HERE, THESE LANDSCAPES-- MEETING LOCALS -- THAT DOES COUNT FOR SOMETHING!

SOME PEOPLE ARE A LITTLE NUTTY, CERTAINLY, BUT THEY'RE SO ENDEARING.

IT'S TRUE THAT WE'VE ALREADY MADE SEVERAL NICE ACQUAINTANCES!

And, as planned, the continuation of the friendships took place that very evening...

~URF!~

PLOP

...with bonds forming already...

OOOWAH, THANKTH! NITHE WAY IN, BUT TOO CHALLENGING FOR ME, I THINK!

SHEE, SHEE, SHEE!

WE'D RATHER YOU ALL CAME IN THROUGH THE WINDOW BECAUSE WE'RE NOT SUPPOSED TO LET YOU COME INTO OUR ROOMS. EVEN YOU AREN'T SUPPOSED TO BE HERE, MARK!

WE'RE THE PRIVILEGED FEW, THEN. I'M FLATTERED!

HEE HEE!

COOL! I WAS A LITTLE AFRAID, BUT YOU SEEM NICE FOR TOURISTS. I HOPE WE'LL SEE EACH OTHER UP THERE.

YOU LOOK REALLY ATHLETIC, FLORIAN. I WAS IMPRESSED WHEN YOU CLIMBED THE WALL EARLIER.

YEAH, I REALLY LIKE CLIMBING!

WHAT ABOUT YOU?

YOU COULD SAY I'M GETTING BY. I MIGHT EVEN DANCE ON THE SLOPES...

The first days' fears soon resurfaced, however...

YOU KNOW, FATOU, JUST HEARING YOU TALKING ABOUT SKIING LAST NIGHT GAVE ME A KNOT IN MY STOMACH!

I'M STRESSING TOO MUCH OVER TOMORROW'S FIRST LESSON!

BE BRAVE! YOU JUST GOTTA GET STARTED.

HA HA HA, CHLOE'S AFRAID OF SKIING! HA HA HA!

~PFF~ DON'T LISTEN TO THAT SNAKE.

It was time for the next place to visit.

PARANNY EDUCATIONAL CENTER, THAT'S NEXT TO VISIT.

CLOSED for repairs

WOW!

COOL!

NOT VERY TRADITIONAL, BUT OKAY!

OKAY... UH... TAKE A LOOK-- BUT JUST FROM OUTSIDE!

MY PROGRAM.

HEH HEH

SO, WE'LL PASS IN FRONT OF IT TO GO TO A SMALL, OLD TRADITIONAL FARM THAT I KNOW, A LITTLE HIGHER UP.

OH, THANKS, THANKS!

TRADITION, THAT'S THE ONLY WORD THEY KNOW IN THESE BOONDOCKS.

THE LITTLE FARM WHERE WE'RE GOING BELONGS TO MARCEL GAILLARD. IT'S VERY DIFFERENT FROM THIS ONE, YOU'LL SEE!

AT LEAST HE LIKES HIS ANIMALS...

SO, THERE ARE TONS OF BADGERS AND STONE MARTENS HERE.

KEEP AN EYE OUT, ANIMALS IN NATURE ARE A GOOD THING. YOU KNOW, NOWADAYS, THIS AREA IS RICH IN BIODIVERSITY AND HAS A GREAT QUANTITY OF SPECIES. SMALL MAMMALS ARE ESPECIALLY ABUNDANT IN THESE PARTS!

THERE'S THE BADGER AND THE MARTEN BESIDE HIM! *HEE HEE!*

YOU HAVE A FREE HAND THIS TIME, MIREILLE!

JACKPOT!

RHAAA!

WHO GOES THERE?

THEY'RE WITH ME, MARCEL! THEY'RE WITH ME-- IT'S OKAY!

HELLO, CLAIRE!

OH, A REAL LOCAL AT LAST!

I KNOW YOU'RE RETIRED NOW, BUT THEY'RE TEMPORARILY CLOSED DOWN BELOW--

SO I THOUGHT I'D BRING MY GROUP TO YOUR PLACE SO THESE KIDS COULD VISIT A MORE TRADITIONAL PLACE.

I'M NOT SURPRISED WITH THEIR INTENSIVE FARMING. ALL RIGHT, THEN, HAVE A LOOK!

THE RIGOR OF THE WINTERS PROMPTED PAST GENERATIONS TO BUILD HOUSES TO DEFY THE AGES. THIS BUILDING IS A GOOD EXAMPLE!

NOWADAYS, HOWEVER, THESE SPACES ARE ABANDONED FOR THE MOST PART.

TOO SMALL AND NOT VERY SPECIALIZED, THEY'VE OFTEN BEEN FORCED TO SHUT DOWN--

HELLO, YOU!

WOOF
WOOF

SIT, GYPSY!

WOOF

With the lessons over, it was time for their lunchbreak...

LUNCH TIME!

THITH THANDWITH ITH ATH HARD ATH A ROCK.

GYPSY DOESN'T AGREE WITH YOU! HEE HEE!

SHE SEEMS TO LIKE YOU! DO YOU LOVE ANIMALS??

YES, I ADORE THEM!

IT'S BEEN A REAL PLEASURE DISCOVERING YOUR REGION. MY FRIENDS AND I EVEN MET THREE PEOPLE OUR OWN AGE FROM HERE!

THAT'S GOOD! YOU'RE NOT LIKE ALL THOSE CITY FOLK WHO ARE AFRAID TO GET THEIR BOOTS DIRTY.

COME THIS WAY, ALL THREE OF YOU. I FEEL LIKE GIVING YOU A TASTE OF MY LEFTOVER STEW.

HMM, YOU LOOK A LITTLE PALE TO ME...

M-- ME?

COME IN, HAVE A LITTLE BITE! COME ON, DON'T MAKE ME ASK TWICE!

I'D BE HAPPY TO SHARE SOME GOOD STEW AMONG FRIENDS.

HEY, THERE! NOT YOU! NO FREE LUNCH!

~MMM~ I LOVE IT!

ABOUT TIME!

TRAVEL JOURNAL

trailblazer special

by Chloe!

Traveling gives you an appetite!
Here's an authentic local dish:

Being authentic
is sooooo
YUMMY

Stew according to Marcel
(and Gypsy)

What kind of "nature" outings
best matches your ideal trip?

You'll need

A shoulder   Cabbage   Potatoes
of pork   Carrots
              Parsley

·Place meat into a stew pot,
cover with cold water and
gently simmer.
·After 1.5 hours, add vegetables
(except potatoes), let simmer
for 30 minutes, then add potatoes,
simmer for 45 minutes.
·Dinner time!   yum!

Simple pleasures, Claire-style

I ♡
Woodchucks!

Volcano Tour

Group Rate
Ticket #020472

Adventures often go along with meeting people.
What message of friendship would
you like to pass along here?

Connections made at last!

Chloe + Romain
Fatouma + Florian
Mark + Pascaline

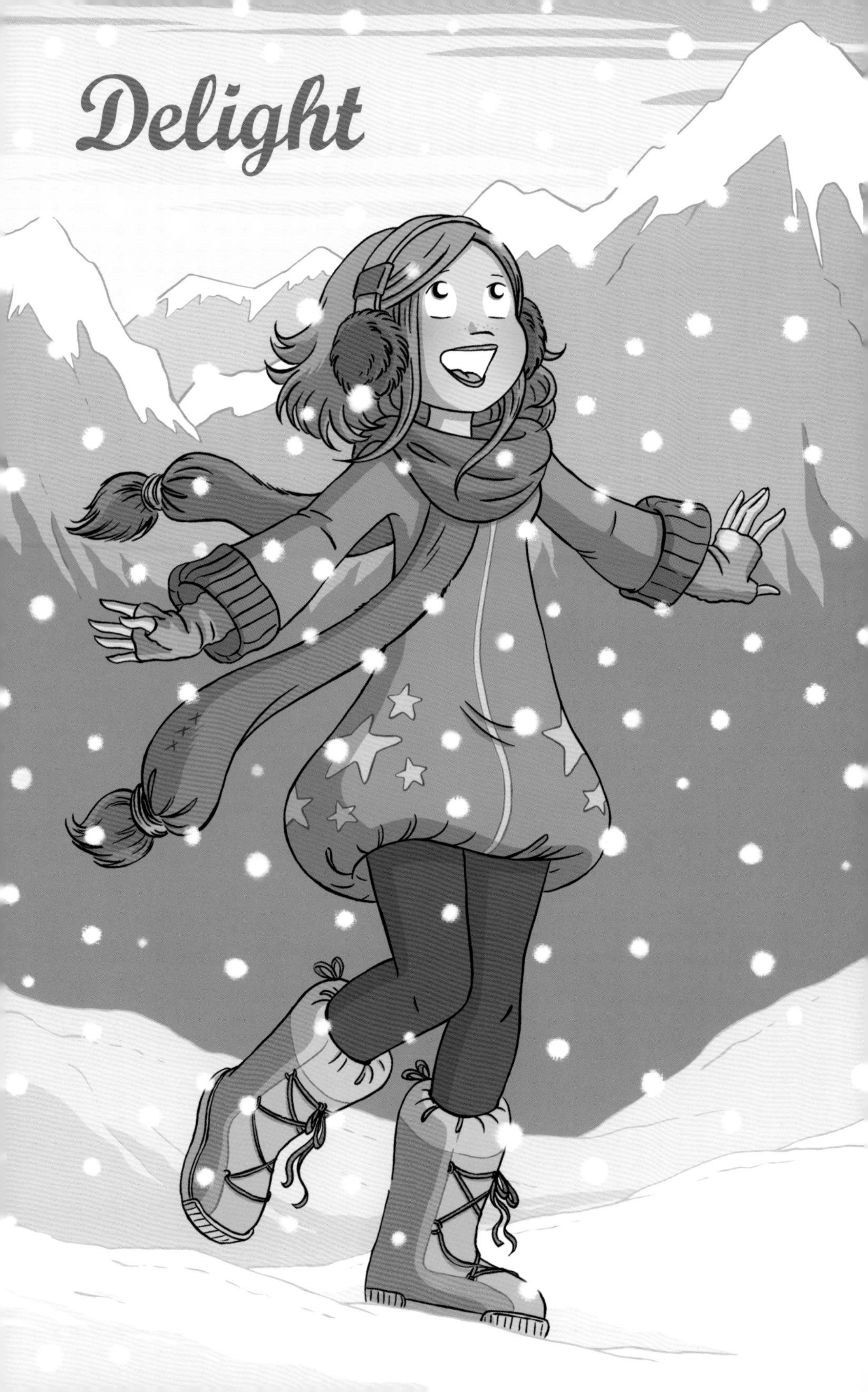
Delight

RENTAL

SO, CHLOE, READY TO LEARN TO SKI NEXT?

MM-- YEAH...

I'LL STAY WITH YOU, SO NO WORRIES. WITH AN OUTFIT AS PRETTY AS YOURS, YOU'LL BE A REAL CHARMER.

YOU THINK SO? HEE HEE!

-PFFF- SHE'S SHOWING OFF WITH HER NEW CLOTHES!

PATHETIC!

UH--YES-- PATHETIC!

OKAY, LESLIE, WE'RE NOT SPENDING THE NIGHT HERE.

IS THIS THE FIRST TIME YOU'VE BEEN SKIING OR WHAT? HA HA HA!

NO, NO, OF COURSE NOT!

-MMFF!- IT WON'T GO ON, TOO BAD!

COME ON, MARK, SHOW A LITTLE SPIRIT! I'M NOBODY'S FOOL!

AND THERE!

SNAP

94

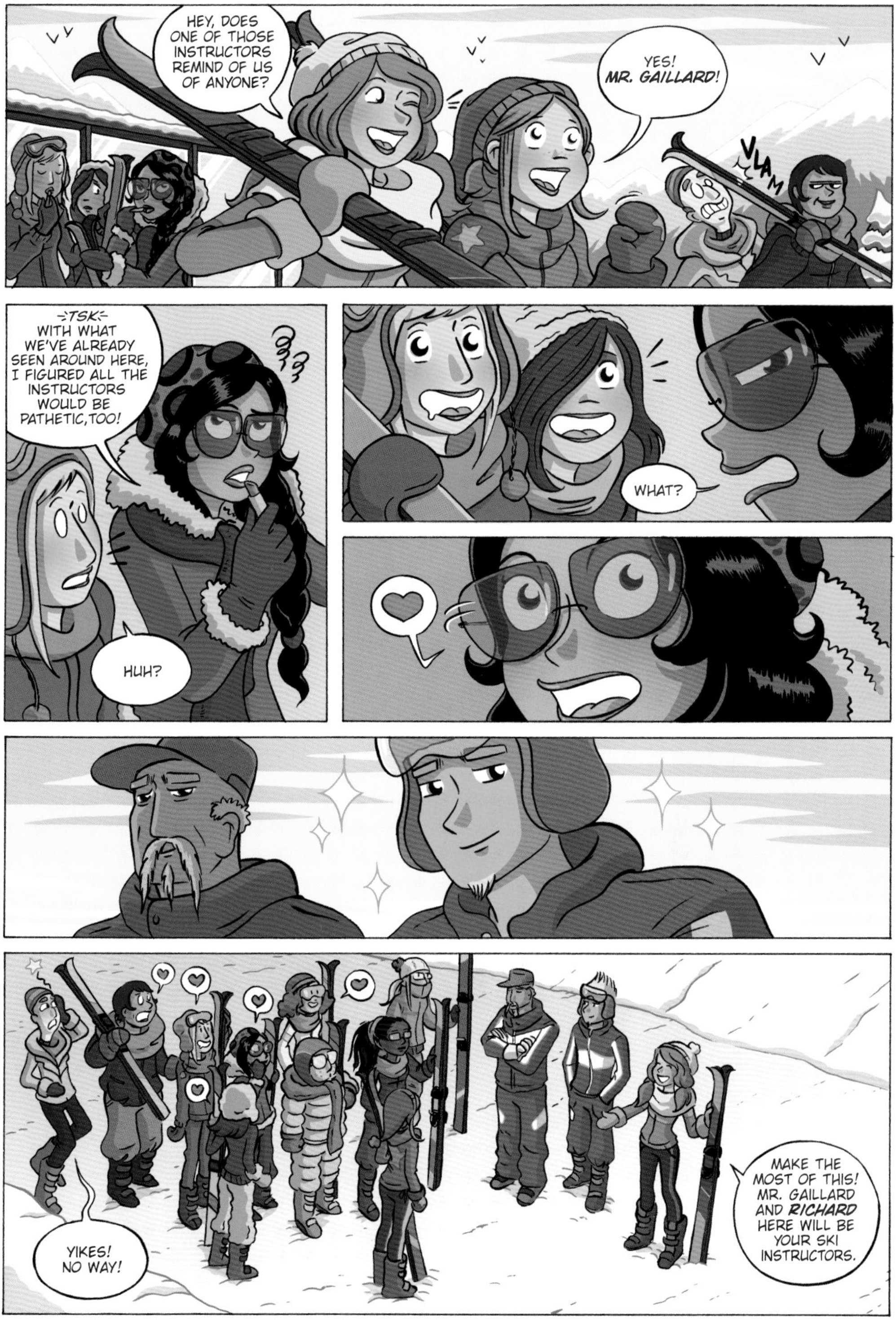
HEY, DOES ONE OF THOSE INSTRUCTORS REMIND OF US OF ANYONE?
YES! MR. GAILLARD!
VLAM
TSK
WITH WHAT WE'VE ALREADY SEEN AROUND HERE, I FIGURED ALL THE INSTRUCTORS WOULD BE PATHETIC,TOO!
HUH?
WHAT?
YIKES! NO WAY!
MAKE THE MOST OF THIS! MR. GAILLARD AND RICHARD HERE WILL BE YOUR SKI INSTRUCTORS.

In Chloe's group, the classes are off to an energetic start...

BEND YOUR KNEES-- YES, LIKE THAT!

THIS IS WRONG. WE WANTED TO BE WITH RICHARD! WE'RE AWESOME SKIERS, AREN'T WE GIRLS?

TOTALLY! I DON'T UNDERSTAND.

I'M NOT GONNA TELL YOU AGAIN. THE GROUPS WERE PICKED AT RANDOM!

UNLUCKY FOR ME-- FORCED TO PUT UP WITH THEM ONCE AGAIN!

WHOA--

YOU REALLY SUCK!

IT'S YOUR FAULT WE'RE NOT SKIING WITH RICHARD!

SHPLOF

EEEEEE!

OKAY, IT'S NO BIG DEAL, GET UP! WE'LL HELP BOTH OF YOU SOME MORE.

HELLO, EVERYONE!

HELLO, CHLOE!

AH, SO YOU'RE THE ONES MY LITTLE PROTÉGÉS MET!

YOU'RE JUST IN TIME! YOU CAN HELP ME TEACH THEM SKIING BASICS!

This new help was very welcome...

YOU SHEE, MARK, TO GO SHLOWER, KEEP YOURSHELF IN A SHNOWPLOUGH POSHISHION!

AAAAAHHH!

?!

ZWIP

HEE HEE HEE! YOU'RE SHO FUNNY!

WOW, YOU'RE DOING BETTER AND BETTER, CHLOE! A REAL SKIER FOR OUR MOUNTAINS. YOU'RE THE BEST!

YOU'RE NOT SO BAD EITHER, YOU KNOW! HEE HEE!

HANG IN THERE, LESLIE, YOU'LL GET IT!

SHE'S NOT GOING TO HANG AROUND THOSE LOSERS NOW!

It was hardly a picnic for the other team either...

LOOK OUT, HERE I COME!

OWW!

OUCH!

UH--AREN'T YOU SUPPOSED TO BE SETTING AN EXAMPLE AND STAYING IN LINE?

I COULDN'T WAIT ANY LONGER! I WANT YOU! KISS ME, YOU BIG FOOL!

HUH? STOP!

LET'S CONTINUE... WE STILL HAVE A LONG WAYS TO GO.

SO THAT'S HOW IT IS! OKAY, YOU'LL SEE WHO'S THE MOST STUBBORN!

That evening, the girls start sharing their first secrets...

DID YOU SEE HOW PASCALINE WAS HANGING AROUND MARK?

YEAH, CRAZY!

AND HE DOESN'T NOTICE A THING EITHER, AS USUAL! HEE HEE HEE!

ANYHOW, I DON'T THINK HE'D BE INTERESTED. VIDEO GAMES ARE MORE HIS THING.

I ALSO THINK ROMAIN HAS A CRUSH ON YOU, CHLOE, DON'T YOU THINK?

NO! YOU'RE KIDDING! HEE HEE!

IF YOU THINK OF HIM SIMPLY AS A FRIEND, DON'T BUILD HIS HOPES UP TOO MUCH, OKAY? IT WOULDN'T BE FAIR TO HIM OTHERWISE.

The next day things became even more delicate...

HEE HEE HEE

OOPS! SORRY, MY LOVE!

SLAP

... sharing was part of it, too!

GO FOR IT?

TOTALLY!

THERE ARE NO BETTER ATHLETES THAN US!

THIS IS THE BEST PROTECTION I'VE EVER HAD IN MY LIFE!

FOR REAL!

One relationship in particular was still very uncomfortable...

I REALLY LOVE SKIING WITH YOU!

OH, UH... YES... UH... ME, TOO, ROMAIN!

OH! UHH... HEY... IT LOOKS LIKE WE'RE HERE!

I CAN'T TAKE IT ANYMORE!

CHLOE, WAIT UP!

?

I WANTED TO ASHK YOU...

YOU KNOW MARK PRETTY WELL. DO YOU THINK HE LIKESH ALL THISH?

HE'SH SHO CUTE!

MAYBE, YES!

UH... LET'S GO JOIN THE OTHERS!

Things had to be made clear...

YOU'VE GOTTEN SOME COLOR THESE PAST FEW DAYS, CHLOE. IT LOOKS GOOD ON YOU!

THANKS, THAT'S SWEET!

I REALLY MEAN IT!

UH-- ROMAIN! YOU KNOW, I DO LIKE YOU--

OH, YEAH, ME TOO!

I LIKE YOU... UH... AS...

--AS A FRIEND, THOUGH!

UH...WELL... YEAH... UH... AS A FRIEND...

OF COURSE, THAT'S... THE SAME FOR ME, TOO... AS A FRIEND, THAT'S RIGHT! YOU ALREADY HAVE A BOYFRIEND-- I KNOW!

...Sometimes you don't need long speeches to make things clear!

BY THE WAY, MARK...

DON'T YOU THINK I'VE CHANGED LATELY?

UH, NO! WHY? YOU'RE THTILL ATH COOL ATH EVER!

The next day got off to an equally difficult start...

MY THKI FELL OFF— WHAT A PAIN!

÷PFFF÷ YOU COULD TRY HARDER, MARK! IT'SH IMPOSHIBLE TO MAKE NO PROGESH IN A WEEK'S TIME?!

HOW ARE YOU LOVEBIRDS?

CHLOE LIKES THE PEASANTS, I GUESS!

BIRDS OF A FEATHER! HA HA HA!

÷PSST!÷ ÷PSST!÷

SORRY!

ACK!

GOOD JOB, LESLIE! YOU'RE FINALLY ONE OF US AGAIN!

YOUR HAT!

WE'LL NEVER GET IT BACK, CHLOE!

PASCALINE'S RIGHT, IT'S TOO DANGEROUS!

DON'T WORRY, WE'LL FIND YOU ANOTHER CAP. THERE ARE TONS LAYING AROUND THE DORM!

BUT IT WAS UNIQUE!

THOSE DARN GIRLS SHOULDN'T GET YOU DOWN.

ALL THREE OF YOU MORE THAN DESERVE A VERY TRADITIONAL TOUR OF MY FARM.

YIPPEE!

OKAY, MY CLASS IS OVER!

CHLOE, CLAIRE, MISS VERNIER, WITH ME! EVERYONE ELSE, NO EXCEPTIONS, WITH RICHARD.

HMMM-- FINALLY!

÷GRRR!÷ NO TOUCHING! HE'S MINE.

ARGH! IT'S CONTINUING--

AND ME?

NO, NOT YET!

Back at Mr. Gaillard's, happiness was the order of the day...

HUH? WHERE ARE WE GOING?

IT'S A SURPRISE! DON'T LAG BEHIND, IT'LL SNOW SOON.

MOOOOO!

OH! SHE'S SO BEAUTIFUL!

THERE'S EVEN A LITTLE CALF!

YES, CHLOE! LET ME INTRODUCE, HIGHNESS, MY ROYAL SALERS COW.

I COULDN'T PART WITH HER.

THAT'S HER CALF JUNIOR BESIDE HER.

LET'S GO TASTE HER HANDIWORK WITH A NICE LITTLE PIECE OF FRESH BREAD.

THIS CHEESE IS SO FRESH!

NOTHING LIKE THIS TO LIFT YOUR SPIRITS!

÷PHEW!÷ IT SMELLS LIKE ROTTEN EGGS!

NOPE! I DON'T HAVE ANY HENS HERE, JUST COWS. HA HA HA!

HEE HEE HEE!

Even if they did have to leave after that, the small pleasures continued outside...

WE'LL MEET DOWN BELOW. NO SPEEDING, OKAY!

AND THANKS AGAIN FOR THE PHONE CALL!

YOU STILL DON'T WANT TO USE MY LANDLINE PHONE TO CALL YOUR PARENTS BEFORE WE LEAVE? I EVEN HAVE INTERNET, YOU KNOW!

NO, THANKS, IT'S OKAY! I'M GOING HOME SOON ANYHOW. I'D RATHER ENJOY THIS LAST EVENING HERE WITHOUT DISTRACTIONS.

YOU SEE, CHLOE, WE CAN CHANGE WITH THE TIMES, WHILE STILL BEING PROUD OF OUR HOMESPUN WAYS AND TRADITIONS!

SOMETIMES WE'RE MODERN, TOO! HA HA HA!

DID YOU SEE?

IT'S SO COOL, ISN'T IT?

÷ACHOO!÷

OH, YES!

WHAT'S MORE, IT LOOKS LIKE LOVE IS IN THE AIR!

IT'S MAGIC!

IT'TH TOO BAD GIRLTH ARE NEVER INTERETHTED IN ME...

THE'TH A KNOCK-OUT!

WHEN MODERNITY AND TRADITION MEET, HEE HEE!

107

TRAVEL JOURNAL

trailblazer special

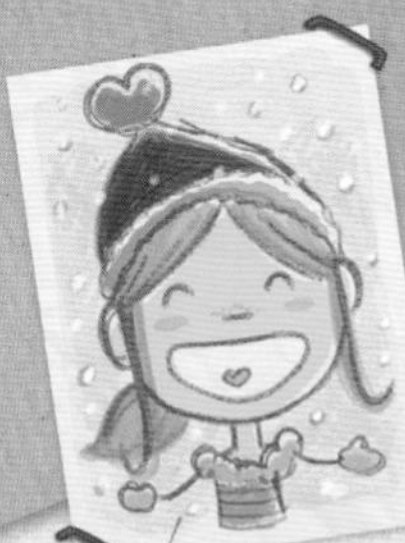

by Chloe!

When you think of "typical" ways of dressing, what comes to mind?

I think of two kinds of clothing, in fact:
* a traditional kind
* a more modern kind

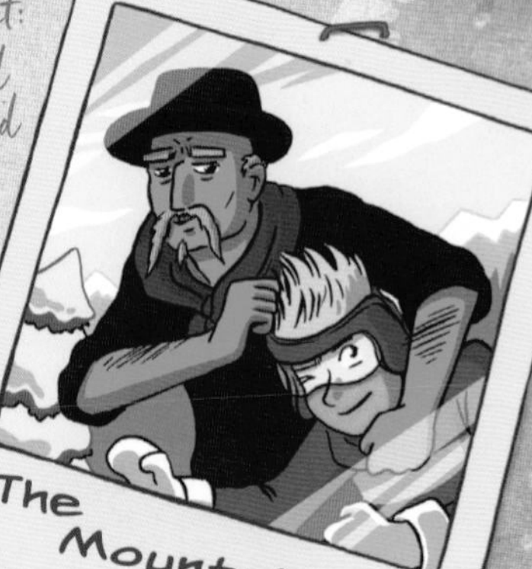

The Mountains Forever

Draw a characteristic animal of those distant lands:

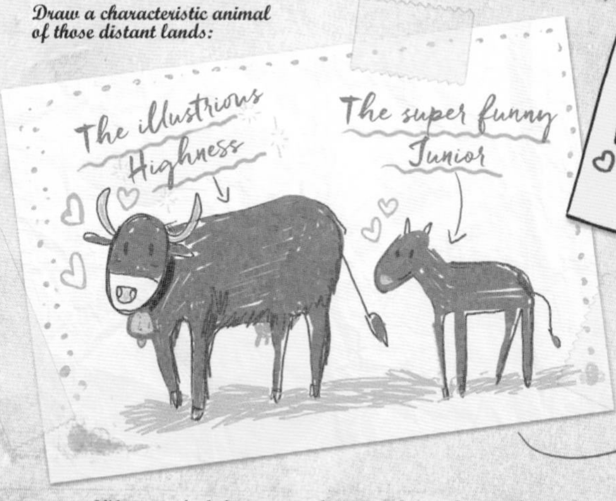
The illustrious Highness
The super funny Junior

Long live Salers cows and their delicious cheese!

What wonderful memories do you want to share right now?

I have so many!
Romain, Claire, Mr. Gaillard, the snow...
Something to totally warm my heart :)
Thank you, Brassens Middle School!

OH, CHLOE! YOU'RE FINALLY HERE!

I THOUGHT I'D NEVER SEE YOU AGAIN!

YOU DIDN'T BREAK ANYTHING, DID YOU?

NO, NO, EVERYTHING'S FINE. WHY WOULDN'T IT BE?

YOUR FATHER DOESN'T WANT TO ADMIT IT, BUT HE WAS TOTALLY LOST WITHOUT YOU!

YOOHOO!

IS THAT TRUE, DAD?

UH... IT'S JUST...

WELL, THEN, MISTER TRAILBLAZER HAD TROUBLE FORGETTING ME! HEE HEE!

WE'LL HAVE TO BE PATIENT A LITTLE LONGER, TONY, BECAUSE I THINK OUR MISTY'S GOING TO ABANDON US FOR A FEW MORE MINUTES!

YEESSS! ALEX!

I MISSED YOU SO MUCH!

NOT AS MUCH AS I DID, BEAUTIFUL!

THE OUTDOORS HAVE MADE YOU LOOK RADIANT!

OH, THANK YOU!

IT WAS AWESOME!

I MET SOME VERY COOL PEOPLE.

THAT'S NOT SURPRISING, HE WAS THERE WATCHING OVER YOU!

WHAT ABOUT MY SNOW, CHLOE. HUH? WHERE IS IT?

IT'S THERE, ARTHUR. JUST OVER YOUR HEAD!

AND THIS...

THIS IS FOR YOU, TOO, FOR LATER... IT'S A JOURNAL FOR GROWING UP!

I'LL GROW UP SOON!

AS TALL AS A MOUNTAIN!

YOUR TEST

Are school field trips right for you?

> TWIN BROTHERS AND FRIENDS, TOO, IT'S AWESOME!

1 You find that a temporary separation from your family is kind of:

❄ Difficult, you're just not used to it.

☆ Stimulating, you're certain new acquaintances will result from it.

◐ Ordinary, you already privilege time with your friends, mostly.

2 During a hike, you prefer the company of:

◐ Your circle of friends, without them it really wouldn't be the same.

❄ Your boyfriend, with him, it can only be magical.

☆ It doesn't matter, above all else, you choose to enjoy the countryside.

> IF A SUCCESSFUL HIKE YOU'D FIND, LEAVE YOUR HIGH HEELS BEHIND! ⇒SNIFF!⇐

> ANYTHING YOU LIKE, BUT NO MORE MOUNTAIN ROADS, PLEASE!

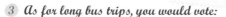

3 As for long bus trips, you would vote:

☆ For, you love traveling.

◐ Against, you hate being inactive.

❄ Neither for nor against; you simply adapt.

4 One of your main qualities might be:

❄ Willpower, you always try to give your best.

☆ Generosity, mainly you hope to share with the greatest number.

☉ Loyalty, your best friends will never really be far from you.

> PERSONALLY, I'D MATCH UP WITH PATIENCE RATHER WELL.

> WE LOVE TABLES FULL OF PEOPLE! DON'T WE, GYPSY?

5 Being around many friends at once is:

☉ An ordeal, you're happy in small groups only.

❄ A concession, you want to make things easier.

☆ A pleasure, you love having people around you.

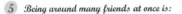

Answers

You mostly have :

Even if it only means being gone for a few days, it's not easy for you to leave your family or your sweetheart either. You're just not used to it, it must be said. You barely left on your school trip, and you're in danger of being overwhelmed with sadness. No worries, however, look carefully around; you're probably not the only one in this situation! So, rely on your courage and determination, they'll make the process of coming together easier. You'll always be happy then.

You mostly have :

You're eager for new experiences. Nothing scares you! You love to travel, ideally in large groups, your greatest satisfaction is in discovering new places. Good for you, you've understood that trips keep a person healthy. So definitely don't hesitate to benefit from that to support friends who may be a bit more uncomfortable than you. By conveying your pleasure to them, you'll lift their spirits and can only come out the better for it.

You mostly have :

Even though you're already independent, your exclusiveness in friendship as well as your horror of crowds won't make you a huge fan of school trips. Because only the presence of your close friends manages to calm your fears, you dread being away from them for very long. In order to best prepare for your trip, try to open yourself up to others more even before your departure. You'll see, thanks to these new experiences, you'll feel less lonely once there! By then sharing these moments with your innermost circle, your bonds can only be strengthened.

> JUST MAKE AN EFFORT AND, I PROMISE YOU, YOU'LL MAKE SOME COOL NEW FRIENDS IN THE END!

> HAPPINESS IS NEVER AS GREAT AS WHEN YOU KNOW THAT IT'S SHARED!

> I CAN TELL YOU YOU ALSHO HAVE LOTSH OF FUN WITH NEW FRIENDSH, *HEE HEE HEE!*